AF334126

MY

DESTINATION

A TRIP TOOK HER TO AN
EXPERIENCE SHE NEVER
EXPECTED

This is a work of fiction. Names, character, places and incidents are either the product of the author's imagination or are used fictitiously, and any resemblance to actual persons, living or dead, business establishments, events or locales is entirely coincidental.

@ COPYRIGHT 2023 BY (CHRISTOPHER WOODWARD)

CHAPTER 1

He looked out of the plane window at the green island approaching rapidly across the sea. Not having travelled much before, the anxiety of flying compounded the uncertainty she felt about the trip. Or more accurately the person she was here to meet.

It had all been so sudden. They had been chatting online for a year, sharing thoughts and experiences, getting to know each other. Finding connections in the little things, despite their lives being so different it was surreal. Him older, her younger, him wealthy, her having no independent means, him needing to control, her wanting to please.

Their chats had become increasingly explicit... and daring. She had succumbed to his influence, becoming increasingly dependent on his opinions, his instructions. Relishing the feeling of obeying him, exposing her to grown-up ideas, of him having his way with her. She had built a grand fantasy about him and what it would be like to be with him.

And now they were meeting, to turn fantasy into reality. But she didn't know him and when he invited her to a villa on the beach, for a few days escape from the drudgery of life, she had said no. Never! She wouldn't do that. Something so foolish, so dangerous. But the fantasy remained, fomenting first in her feelings and then in her thoughts. Maybe it wouldn't be so bad. He seemed nice enough. But what if he was a psychopath or a trafficker? Even thinking about it made her wet with trepidation and anticipation, her panties soaking and her pussy tingling.

Until she said 'yes'. And here she was, landing on the exotic island. She had never even dreamed that she would be in such a place, in such a situation. Her past a traumatic place, leaving her distrusting and doubtful. But, also at the mercy of her needs, her wants, her darkest desires.

They had messaged each other about the psychology of domination, both the perpetrator and prey. She felt like a little bird, injured and trying to mend, wanting care, fearful of submission, but needing something darker and more frightening to affirm her. To satisfy her craving, to quench her passion.

To be desired unconditionally, wanted irresistibly. To gain a semblance of control by losing it to a man's uncontrollable lust for her. Where he would surrender himself in the act of domination and thereby lose a part of himself that he held dear. She was scared and excited, overwhelmed by the experience and what might be, her emotions tossed like a small bird in a violent storm.

He stood there, waiting. Looking just like his profile. Unperturbed by the chaos of people around him, eyes only for her. A calm in the maelstrom that is an airport arrivals hall. Standing tall, tanned and trim from hours on the ocean. His untucked white collared shirt, blue jeans and black boardriders, an image of casual elegance, juxtaposed against the cacophony of boardshorts, teeshirts and sandals around him.

Grey blue eyes, watching her approach, boring into her soul, not letting her resist, but sending a flutter of insecurity through her stomach. Heart racing, she hesitantly walked up to him, as he appraised her top to bottom. Her light brown silken hair pulled back in a ponytail for the flight, framing a pretty face with delicate feminine features, small upturned nose and slightly pouting lips. The tight yellow spaghetti-strap top emphasising her small pert breasts and her dainty arms, which he took in with a smile. A short denim skirt revealing her shapely slender legs balancing on three-inch wedge shoes. The outfit screaming 'I'm on holiday!'

Uncertain, she held out a hand to greet him, not knowing whether to give him a peck on the cheek. Instead, he took her suitcase, grabbed her hand and commanded "Come! I want to get out of here."

He walked fast, used to moving through airports like a salmon upriver, hating the crowds and the noise. She tottered along after him, unused to the brisk pace in her heels, his firm grip controlling, pulling, wrenching her arm. At one stage she tripped, but he just pulled her up not letting her fall, but not stopping.

Her hand was sore from his grip and her shoulder throbbed from the strain. When she mumbled "Wait? I can't walk that fast." He just sped up, saying nothing and not looking back at the girl in his wake.

And then they were at his SUV, where without saying a word he packed her case in the back. Feeling lost and dishevelled, she looked up at him towering over her, questioning and suddenly afraid. Those intense eyes searching again, making her feel like prey.

Grabbing her ponytail, he kissed her hard, bruisingly hard - lips grinding, tongues duelling, teeth nibbling, him owning. She responded by submitting, reacting, allowing, letting him take what he wanted. Her body contoured into his and she felt the familiar tingle in her loins and her pebble hard nipples rubbing against his hard chest.

And then as suddenly as he started, he stopped and opened her door, guiding her in before going around to the driver's side. Instantly the gentleman. She said nothing. Just glancing at him with timid eyes, before looking forward. What could she say? He had brought he here. She had come willingly. Was this a bad idea? The three-quarter-of-an-hour drive to the cottage on the north shore was wonderful. He was caring and engaged, talking about her life and current situation, small events that had caused her irritation or joy. He shared his travel experiences, making light conversation and sharing amusing anecdotes.

His hand strayed onto her knee, where it stayed, making little circles while he talked. She pushed it away twice, but each time it returned, gentle but insistent, staying on her knee so she gave up and succumbed to the sensual feeling of light fingers trailing over her skin.

Initially the stark volcanic mountains rising out of tropical green island reflected in the turmoil of her emotions. But soon she felt safe and secure, a soft glow permeating from her heart into her tummy. Blue of the glassed ocean reflecting her mood as they pulled into the small cottage on the beach.

He showed her in, depositing the cases inside the door. She was caught by surprise as he grabbed her ponytail and pushed her roughly against the hallway wall. She resisted murmuring "Hey. What're doing?"

He responded by silently shoving her harder, her shoulder bruising on the hard surface. Only a low warning growl in her ear, like a wild animal. Communicating his intent without words. Pulling her spaghetti top up, exposing her pert breasts, which he mauled with unbridled lust. He tweaked her dusky pink nipple, the suddenness of it pushing past the point of pleasure into sharp pain. Chuckling at her sharp cry, he told her to "Get used to it!". His other hand found its twin nub, trapped between her and the wall, he twisted them, sending jolts of pleasure-pain down between her legs.

That attention brought the shocking realisation that she was sopping wet. But he had no right to take what he wanted. So, she pushed back pleading "It's too soon. Let's talk and get to know each other in person. I want to find out about more you. Please?"

He responded by pressing his hard manhood against her, cradling it into her arse, pulling down on her nips, making her arch her back and rub her butt against his groin. A moan of pleasure from him and a groan of frustration from her. "Stop!" Again, she tried to push back, but she was too weak, and he too determined.

Grabbing her hair, he shoved her up against the rough wall.

CHAPTER 2

She could see the uneven plaster work, feel the smooth cool paint, smell the dust of the wall as her face was pushed against it, keeping her immobile, at his control. Why was she studying the wall, when she was about to be abused? Was it rape? If she came all this way willingly? Was this fantasy or reality? Did it matter? He twisted her torso through the grip on her pony to arch her back. Lifting her short denim skirt, he exposed her flimsy pink panties. It was saucy underwear that he had bought her, made her buy online for him. Why did she wear it? It gave no protection, as he demonstrated by grabbing it and pulling it over her tight round buttock, giving her a hard slap while telling her to "Shut the fuck up and take it! I know what you want."

He loved the way his handprint blossomed on her pearl white skin. She hated the sting and the callous way he stuck a couple of fingers into her soaking slit taunting, "A needy slut aren't you. You're loving this no matter what you say."

She heard the popping of buttons on his jeans. Felt his feet kicking her ankles apart, his hardness trailing over her backside, leaving a light moist trail across her skin. And then in an instant of brutality, he thrust his entire organ between her legs and into her core, drawing a shocked gasp followed by a hesitant moan as she felt the fullness she craved.

He had said it would feel like this their first time. Memorable, passionate and intense, but she hadn't realised this is what he meant. She'd had visions of gentle lovemaking in soft sheets, not a rough fucking at the front door. Then why did her body feel so responsive, betraying her?

But that didn't stop her resisting. She tried to wriggle out of his grasp, but only managed to scrape her cheek and breast. Like the time she had fallen and grazed herself. When she had told him about it, he helped her treat it, but said that sometimes one just has to 'suck it up' and deal with the pain. She hadn't understood then, but he said that she would, eventually. His grip too strong, as he ignored her "Please. Not like this!"

But now she was not sure if she meant it or it was part of the sick game they were playing. Not knowing where fantasy and reality met. Her body didn't care as her arousal grew and her pussy flooded the manhood plumbing her depths.

He pounded her then, leaning on her back, her tits rubbing against the wall. Nipples darkening from lust and the abrasion, until they were so sensitive that the pain and pleasure collided, and still he would not stop, riding her, hand in her hair, pulling her back onto him. In control. Or was he? Was he at the mercy of his dark desires, his body responding, instinctively, just like hers?

He grabbed her chin, strong hands encircling her neck and twisting her head until she was looking at him over her shoulder. He continued rutting into her, building the pleasure between her legs, searching for the precipice that she hoped to fall over, but still she snarled for him to stop. Even as she rocked back onto his cock.

His unshaven stubble rubbed her cheek, scraping her sensitive skin, before he kissed her again, like before, rough and forceful, dominating her small mouth. Biting harder now on her lips and tongue, not drawing blood but drawing pain and confusion from her hormone-addled mind.

Pleasure and pain converging, resistance and submission blending under his tutelage. His hand thrust down the front of her panties to strum her clit, alternating between gentle flicks and intense pinches. In time with his cock slipping seamlessly in and out of her, until he knew she was falling over the edge of an intense orgasm. The first she had ever experienced on a real live cock.

With a hard nip on her engorged nub, he flooded her insides, the sensations causing explosions in her loins, in her gut, in her chest and in her head, as all of her sensations overloaded, and she lost track of time and space in the small death of her climax.

And still he pounded deep and hard, depositing every last drop of his seed within her and extracting his own pleasure from her writhing, clasping body.

A little while later they were lying together on a daybed on the porch, in the late afternoon sun. He was his charming self again, contrite but not apologetic. Rubbing cream onto her breasts to sooth the abrasions to her nipples, arnica on her bruises, sensitively kissing every one. Trying to heal his little bird who had come through the storm, battered, but intact, until the next time.

"Why'd you do that? Why hurt me?" She asked timidly, hoping not to anger him but wanting to know. "You said I would remember the first time. It would be special."

"You will remember it." He looked into her eyes intently, boring into her soul. "For most people the first time is boring, like vanilla desert. Lying humping. Missionary. Nothing memorable."

He caressed her breasts and pinched the sensitive nipple, asking "How does this feel?"

"Sore."

"Is that all? It's hard as a rock." He rubbed the abrasions left on the pale skin by the rough wall. "You liked it. Didn't you? It made you feel alive. Wanted. No boundaries."

The way he looked at her, exposing her deepest thoughts, her darkest desires. She couldn't lie. "Y-y-yes."

"And here, where I slapped you." He grabbed her butt cheek, hard enough for her to feel the bruise, deep in the muscle. "How'd that feel?"

She couldn't deny the surge of moisture in her pussy before, and now. "Good... I think."

"What happened? Good how?" He insisted.

"It made me wet." Hesitantly, feeling emotionally naked and spread open before him, just like her physical body on the daybed. "But it hurt. It stung." A spark of resistance. Trying not to lose herself in his logic, his probing eyes.

"Life is all about extremes. Living large." He chided, talking to her like she was a child. "We harness these extremes to feel alive. Pleasure and pain, two sides of love." He paused to let his words sink in. "Only children want pleasure the whole time. They don't know the truth."

CHAPTER 3

She looked up at him confused, about to say something, but he cut her off. "I loved that you gave me your body, entirely. The greatest gift a woman can give to a man. I'm so proud of you. You made me happy. I felt your pain. You squeezed me so tight when I was inside you. I felt every shock, every jolt. Felt you clenching on me. . . to make me feel good. . . like you should."

He kissed each nipple, flicking it gently with his tongue, sending tremors through her core, lighting her loins, flooding her slit. "That's why I put soothing cream on them afterwards, to show how much you mean to me. I want you to be whole, to mend you. So, you can give yourself to me again. Pure."

His tongue traced down her stomach, sending involuntary spasms through her gut and into her pussy, making it tingle with anticipation. But he then kissed a trail around to her buttocks where he softly blew on the discoloured flesh, causing goose bumps. "And it's why I rubbed oil here, to take away the pain. Because I care."

The sensations surging through her young body, the chaos of her emotions and the seductive tone of his voice bewildered her, making her doubt herself, her thoughts, her feelings. . . But in a way that felt 'oh so good'. Maybe he was right. Maybe it was okay. She was sure that he did care. And yes, it was memorable... even if she hurt... but it was for him.

"You have a beautiful body. Perfect in every way." He was stroking her, caressing all over, gently, lovingly. "It was meant to be used. In every way. That's why I made you use the hairbrush. So, you were ready for me."

He had first seen her on Periscope, flashing her breasts. He PM'ed her warning her not to do that, there may be predators on the internet and that got them talking. At first, he told her nothing about himself, but used the shy arousal he had seen that first time to push her. When they were eventually talking about meeting up, he had got her to masturbate with increasingly large items, from pens up to her hairbrush handle. Making her break her own hymen on video for him at one stage.

Even though she cried a bit, he told her she was a 'good girl' and let her buy a gift using the e-wallet he had set up on her smartphone. The gift was sexy lingerie that he later got her to model for him on video feed, a win-win as far as he was concerned.

"But I said 'no'. I asked you to stop." Whispered, in a last attempt to hold onto that part of herself. Her control. "You should have waited until I was ready. Like you said you would."

He chuckled then. A deep dark sound that she hadn't expected. "My innocent little bird. You belong to me now. You came to me, to give yourself. To ME. This body is mine, to play with. When I want! How I want! Where I want!" He paused, before growling. "Because you need this. Because you were born for me. To give me pleasure with your body. To be my canvass. Because you're a hot little slut. . . Oh, you were definitely ready."

He had stopped kissing her sore parts and kneeled up above her. An indecipherable smirk flitting across his mouth, but not into his eyes. His eyes now hard, impaling her with their coldness, their intensity. Making it so she could not move, could not breathe. She could hardly think, bewildered and vulnerable.

"This mouth is mine!" He leaned down and kissed her, deep and rough, tongue deep into her throat, ravaging her teeth, her tongue, his teeth biting her lips, drawing blood with a particularly hard nip, which he licked away as he pulled back.

"These tits are mine!" He grabbed them hard, squeezing the flesh, hurting them. Like he had said he would in their internet chats. Telling her that it would feel like the time she was hit in the chest by a softball, so hard it bruised for a week.

Twisting the nipples, making them burn. Like when he had made her put clothes pegs on them while they chatted. Making her pinch them herself, to show her obedience. But never as hard as this. She couldn't do that to herself. Confused at how it made her pussy feel, pain shooting down between her legs making her wet, horny, bewildered.

This ass is mine!" Spanking her, on the bruises. Alternating with a slow sensual massage, increasing pressure until it hurt, followed by another slap on the same place, over and over until her skin was red and each slap stung that much more. Making her gush, shamelessly. Is this how a slut responded?

"This cunt is mine!" Not even turning her over. Just sliding his thumb down her ass crack to her slit. Plunging it in. Into the sopping maw. Up to the wrist. Not pumping. Just writhing it around in her, making her shiver in ecstasy as he rubbed her sweet spot in the passage, deep within. Warmth emanating through her body to crash into the electric pulses from her nipples, as he still casually twisted them in time with his thumb's movements.

His fingers slipping forward along her pussy lips, making them swell. Reaching the clit in expectation, but then pushing back the hood to expose the small nub. Pinching it, hard between the nails of his middle fingers. Sending shockwaves of pain-pleasure into her gut, to meet the rolling warmth from her g-spot.

Her body a tumult of sensations, a tsunami washing over it. Stripping away her pretence. Submitting to what he was doing. What he wanted.

"You never say 'no' to me... Ever." Whispered. His gentle voice contrasted with the force and depth of his remarks. Searing into her memory as a lifelong reminder of his domination. Turning her over, raising her legs by the ankles, into a wide V, snarling "Keep them up."

In her uncertainty, she had not seen how hard he was. His manhood standing proud, hard and ready. Holding her legs behind the calves, opened for him, for his pleasure. At his command. Plunging into her waiting quim. It was ready for him to take what he wanted. Exploding around him with her arousal, two thrusts and she was cumming like a wanton whore.

CHAPTER 4

He took her there, the way he wanted, looking down at her, the predator toying with the prey. She submitted, her body his to play with, to make her feel things she had never felt before. Orgasms, crashing on her, like waves on the shore, unending, pulsating, devastating.

He grabbed her ankles again, pushing them besides her head, stretching her. Doubled up as he pounded into her, all her muscles and sinews straining, making her tight for him. Her discomfort, his pleasure. But it still didn't stop her needy cunt from cumming for him, on his hard manhood.

And then it was over, when he was done. Not in her pussy like she expected, but rather in her mouth. Straddling her chest, cock shiny with her juices and his precum. Holding her head tight by the hair, so that his glans was resting on her lip as he shot streams of thick salty seed onto her tongue. Coating her mouth with the very first layer of man cum she had ever tasted.

Trying not to retch with the unfamiliar taste. Wiping the head off on her cheek as he told her to swallow. She looked up, perplexed. But obeyed, or at least tried to. Three times, each time her throat rebelling at the texture and the smell. Eventually getting it down, but traces all around the inside of her cheeks, permeating her nostrils. And then his cock was back in as he told her to clean him off.

"Come. I want to show you around." He had put on a beach gown, but not given her one. She tried to cover herself as he pulled her up by the arm, but he slapped her hands away. "You are beautiful. Be proud of your body. I want to see all of you."

He took her firmly by the hand and walked her out past the sparking blue pool in front of the 2-bedroom villa, towards the beach. She saw people walking along the beach in front of the solid wooden fence, but fortunately none of them looked up. He put his arm possessively around her, stroking her shoulder down to her breasts, which he cupped gently, his calloused fingers rubbing her tender flesh while using his thumb to thrum her sensitive nipple.

She realised that her nakedness was hidden from the people on the beach, but not the next-door villa. She could not make anything out through the darkened windows but imagined someone looking out and seeing her exposed. The blush of humiliation coloured her neck and sent a burst of energy into her pussy. Why was she always so wet, since she had arrived here with him? She couldn't stop it. And she was no longer sure she wanted to.

"I'll take you to the beach tomorrow, but tonight we are going out." He turned and led her back into the house, guiding her into a room with a view of the sea, open to the en suite bathroom. "This is your room. I've bought you some clothes and some make up. Clean up and put on the clothes I take out for you. I want you looking elegant this evening. Understand?"

His look left her no choice but to obey, so she nodded and went into the shower. When she had finished, he was gone. A little backless black dress with 3-inch gold stiletto heels were laid out on the bed. No underwear.

She saw her suitcase in the corner and opened it to get some panties, because the dress wouldn't allow a bra. She noticed that her computer hard drive and her smartphone were gone. He had told her to bring the drive so that no one could find out that they had been chatting. She got the smartphone so that he alone could use it to contact her, through various chat channels. It was also how she paid for the things he wanted to buy her, using e-wallet and electronic recharging. She thought that it was strange that they were missing and decided to ask him about it later.

Selecting her favourite lacy black thong, that felt so sensual against her bare mound, she put on the dress and heels and tied her hair up in a messy bun, leaving a few tendrils framing her face, which she made up with judicious use of the cosmetics.

He had sent her to a salon to learn about make up a couple of months before, where they taught natural, sophisticated to party looks. It was one of the increasingly stringent demands he had made of her over the past six months, ensuring that she would look good for him. Like the sexy clothes and lingerie that he made her buy and model for him, streaming through her cam, even though she couldn't see him. It always puzzled her why he wouldn't let her see him when she had to perform for him, like an anonymous voyeur.

Lately she had been told to undress for him, acting like a stripper swaying to music he chose and slowly revealing her underwear. And then masturbating with her hairbrush in front of the camera, showing him what a 'good girl' she was. Always cumming, hard and intense, reinforced by her embarrassment at acting so lewdly and his voice complimenting her on how beautiful she looked.

This too was puzzling, because she had never been able to orgasm by herself before he started watching her. Her body responding subconsciously to the shame of such a private act, performed on camera for him. Not knowing whether he was recording her and what he would do with such a video, but still not being able to resist his commands.

She had begun to see her orgasms at belonging to him. He had taught her how to find that sensitive spot deep inside her vagina, to really find it and give herself that deep pleasure that it provided. From him, she explored the ways to make her clit come alive, to stroke it gently at the start and then increase the speed and pressure as it enlarged and became oh so sensitive. Until she felt her heart was going to explode with the sensations shooting up through her gut.

Desperate for his praise and the warm feeling it gave her, being affirmed and acknowledged. The words 'good girl' always triggering a flush of pleasure through her body. Being told she was pretty, encouraged her to try and look good, act sexy. To do whatever he asked.

CHAPTER 5

Making herself up for him now made her tingle down there, like it always did, triggering those thoughts and her psychological associations. She had even felt it, when based on his instruction, she had made herself up to look older for the flight, in order to match her false ID.

He had made her go to a seedy part of town to a forger, to get the false drivers permit, under a false name and birthdate that he had selected, to indicate that she was twenty-one. The thin creepy guy never stopped ogling her, making her feel very uncomfortable. Taking the bus there, she felt so vulnerable, so exposed, so at risk. She felt so dirty after the ordeal that she had to take a shower when she got home.

But she also felt a strange excitement from the danger, the sense that she could be forced to do something by unknown men. She frigged herself to a crashing orgasm in the shower and had to relay the whole ordeal and her thoughts and feelings of the experience to him later that night, leaving her horny all over again. But that time he forbade her to touch herself, or later in bed. She spent the whole night frustrated, tossing and turning, but not disobeying. Being a 'good girl'.

He was reclining in the lounge when she was ready. Subtle lighting casting pools across the room, leaving him in partial shadow as the evening extinguished the light from outside. She walked over towards him, feeling self-conscious in the extremely short dress and high heels. She was aware that the loose front would allow any watcher a tantalising view of her breasts if she leant forward, so she was subconsciously holding her shoulders back and thrusting her hardened nipples forwards creating two small spikes through the thin material.

"Stand here," Pointing to a spot besides his armchair. Looking at her with an unfathomable expression, he slid a hand up her thigh, possessively reaching her panty clad crotch.

"What's this? I didn't put this out." He growled, fiercely squeezing her pussy lips through the material, between thumb and forefinger, causing a jolt of pain.

"I thought. . ." She stammered.

"Don't think. Do what I say." He interrupted, roughly grabbing her arm and pulling her over his lap. Sliding the short dress up to expose her thong split buttocks. He spanked her hard and fast, ten blows causing red blossoms to bloom on her skin. Too choked up and surprised to cry out, she took it silently, except for the resounding crack that shattered her hearing as his hand met her bruised flesh. The double pain ratchetting through her body like a forest fire.

"Do you understand?" Pushing her down onto her knees in front of him he demanded. "What have you got to say?"

"I'm s-s-sorry." Trembling lip, only just holding back the waterworks

"And?" Merciless

"I w-w-won't d-do it again." Hoping that's what he was asking for. Thinking of nothing else except stopping his anger. Asking his forgiveness. Contrite, on her knees in supplication before him. "Please. . ."

"Alright. Since you want them on, you can keep them on." Relief at his words "For now." What does that mean? But she didn't have the courage to resist him or question him. "Are you going to be my 'good girl'?"

"Yes. . . Thank you. Sir." It just felt right to call him that. To thank him.

He got up, taking her hand and pulling her up gently then. The contrast more than her brain or her heart could bear. She just wanted him to be like this. Caring. She was certain that she'd do anything to ensure that he stayed like this. She'd be a 'good girl'. His 'good girl'. Whatever it took.

They were in the car when he told her cryptically. "I have so much to show you. Starting tonight." He had been driving in silence, his hand up her thigh, caressing the soft skin just below her crotch, but never touching her. Driving her wild in anticipation, feelings of frustration and shame colliding, as he aroused her while taking liberties without asking

The valet took the car when they got to where they were going. A jazz and dinner club, with a dance floor, and people who danced like they were on TV. She felt panic, never having danced like that before. Was he going to make her?

Leading her to their reserved table, on the edge of the room against the wall but with a clear view of the dancers. He chivalrously held out the chair for her to sit down, casually flipping the back of the dress as she did, so that her sensitive and bruised bare cheeks met and rubbed against the velvet seat, making sure she was continually reminded of her discomfort and his domination earlier that night. She sat, initially surprised and then understanding as he pushed her shoulders down when she tried to tuck the dress under her.

He ordered for her, a salad and a glass of white wine, not asking what she wanted, rather deciding what she would get. She had never really had wine before, but she knew not to refuse when he toasted to her beauty. The sip burst on her tongue and into her stomach, warming her.

"Give me your panties." Out of the blue. "I wanted you bare, so now you'll do what I wanted."

She looked at him in horror. "What?"

"You heard me. I know you're wet." He taunted her quietly. "Sluts don't get to wear panties." Waiting a few seconds, while she stared at him, petrified. "Come on, I'm going to count to ten."

"Please can I go to the bathroom?" She couldn't comprehend taking them off here. Now that he had mentioned it, she felt her own wetness and was dying of shame. How could her body betray her like this?

"No. Here. Now. . . One. . . Just slip your thumbs under your skirt and slip them down. . . Two. . . You don't want to make me angry again. . . Three. . . Do you?" He was smiling patiently, enigmatically.

CHAPTER 6

That got her moving. She had told herself she would do anything to be his 'good girl'. With the skirt bunched up at the back it was easy to slide the hand nearest the wall up to the string over her hip, pushing it down and wriggling her bottom to slide it underneath. "Four. . ." But the other side wouldn't slide, she'd have to push it too, in front of everyone. She looked around blushing crimson and did it, for anyone to see. Until she had the thong stretched tight across her thighs.

"Five. . . Good, now take them off. No one is looking. . . Six." Only four to go. Down to her knees under the table. That was easy. "Seven. . ." Raising her right leg. Slipping if off past her ankle and her shoe under the table. "Eight. . ." Raising the other leg. Oh no, it's stuck on the heel. Please no. At last, it's off.

"You'd better hurry. . . Nine. . . Put it in my hand." He held out his hand, cupped in the middle of the table. The waiter was coming back. Would be at the table in five seconds. She couldn't. . . She had to. She looked down and quickly placed the crumpled material in his hand, keeping it covered as the waiter came up with their mains. Hiding it as if holding his hand.

"Let the man put your plate down." He smiled sardonically, staring at her until she reluctantly withdrew her hand, to her lap. Not being able to look anywhere except at her plate. Crimson shame pulsing through her cheeks. She could see that he had not moved his hand, the garment sitting there like an accusation. Telling everyone she was a slut. Who else would do such a thing?

"Let's eat." He slipped the thong into his pocket as the waiter left. "I expect you are sopping. I hope you don't make a mess of the chair."

He was right. Her traitorous pussy was swampy. She tried to clench her kegel muscles and her thighs to prevent it from soiling the seat. Picking at the salad, distracted, horny. Feeling her lust bubbling up. Threatening to consume her.

He chatted, unconcerned with her struggles, her suffering, her mortification. Enjoying the music, the food and her beautiful desperation. She ate too but didn't taste the salad. She drank the wine and it relaxed her, made her more accepting of her fate.

Standing suddenly, he held out his hand and walked her onto the dance floor. She wanted the ground to swallow her up, knowing that a sudden swing or fall would expose her breasts or her womanhood to everyone. In in her slightly inebriated state, she was sure that would happen. And she could feel her squelching uncovered slit as she walked, juices dampening her inner thighs.

But he didn't let her fall. Rather he held her firmly and led her around the floor, as if she had been dancing for years. Caressing her back, whispering how beautiful she was. How much she turned him on. His hand slipping down the back of her loose dress, onto her backside, against her naked skin. She couldn't help thrusting her hips into his groin, her nipples onto his chest.

Flooded with sensations, incapable of resisting this man who had taken control of her, and her life. As they danced, she felt droplets of moisture ooze from her slit, dripping down between her thighs, making them embarrassingly slick as she moved, which just made her body naturally juice more.

Back at the table he whispered to her "I want you to drop your napkin, and when you reach for it, expose your tit and shove it into my hand. I want to fondle you." He draped his hand off the table in front of her, palm up. On the restaurant side of the table, where anyone could see. His eyebrow raised, waiting.

She didn't know what to say. This was too much. "Please. . ." She said nothing more, because she didn't know what she was asking. "If you don't listen, I might just leave you here." The fire in his eyes showed his determination. "You can work out how to get back, if you even know where the villa is."

The threat struck a cold desperation deep in her gut, clasping her heart in a tight grip, making it hard to breathe. She couldn't let that happen. She couldn't imagine the consequences. She didn't know where the villa was, the street address or even what it was called. Without thinking, she dropped her napkin, bent down and slipped her hand across her front to pull the top aside. As her tit popped out, she aimed it at his hand to fill it with the soft flesh, frowning in concentration, in humiliation, in arousal.

The first time he ever saw her, twelve months earlier, he was flipping through Periscope chats. He would occasionally browse those video chats for titillation, looking for chicks who were exposing themselves. It always amazed him how easy it was to get them to take off their clothes on camera, for a few likes or gifts.

He loved the indirect control of manipulating them into doing things they would never do in real life. For him, it didn't matter who they were, the control was what he liked.

And then there she was. This gorgeous, innocent looking, woman. Chewing her lip pensively, reading the posts. It seemed that a few commenters had been bullying her. Telling her they were going to leave the chat if she didn't do something interesting. Show them something. A common theme about exposing herself for them. Various comments like, 'lift your top' and then 'a gift if you show us your titties.' She had resisted initially, but now seemed to be considering it. Asking that they follow her, obviously wanting affirmation and searching for attention.

She hesitated and then with a demure glance at the camera, she did. Showing the world her pert breasts with their dusky puffy nipples. The same look, concentrating on the words on the chat, hints of shame at her act and the beginnings of arousal as she realised that she was probably turning on the men that were watching. The neediness and the willingness to please, making him pause and engage her through PM, drawing her in by 'protecting' her from predators. . .

He relished the same look now, as she thrust herself on him in desperate compliance. That felt almost as good as the firm flesh in his hand, which he groped mercilessly, adding a wince to her facial expressions. But like a good girl, she didn't pull away, just accepted the treatment he dished out.

CHAPTER 7

She only straightened when he released her tit and withdrew his hand with a "Good girl. I'm pleased with you." The surge of pride she felt at those words made it all worthwhile.

When they were preparing to leave, he looked down at the wet spot that had stained the chair seat, telling her to clean her slutty mark. He waited while she used the napkin, bending over with his hand on her backside, trying to dry it. Dying with shame as he casually told the waiter that she was just cleaning some food she had dropped.

Later when they were in the car, he said "You've got me all worked up. Lean over and suck me, while I take you home." The nonchalant entitlement shocked her. But she was in no position to resist. As she took him into her mouth, to give her very first proper blowjob he instructed. "Just like I taught you on that dildo."

She cringed at the thought. It was one of her worse purchases at his direction. He made her go to a horrible adult shop, full of lecherous men and tattooed goth women. She had to buy an eight-inch black dildo, a pink vibrator and a silver princess butt plug. She knew about these things in theory, but never expected to see them, much less own such things.

Over the next weeks, he had introduced her to the joys or in her view the shame and pain of using them. He was most insistent on the dildo, making her suck it for what seemed like hours, until three months later, she could competently take the entire thing into her mouth and down her throat.

Now she used her lessons to good effect and was quickly bobbing in his lap as he drove, taking him entirely in and using her tongue like a seasoned whore to caress the shaft. As he got close, he would tap her head and she would slow down. A trick that he had taught her virtually, pretending the dildo was him and she was responding to his active involvement.

Eventually he allowed her to take him over the top as he drove into the driveway of the villa, unloading down her throat to deliver his second batch of semen into her stomach.

Later, lying in her bed she couldn't sleep. The itch between her legs wouldn't go away. Despite being driven to frenzied arousal all evening, he hadn't touched her once after they got home. And he forbade her to touch herself. The feelings of desperation and helplessness that she had to endure just made her hotter and hornier.

It wasn't just the frustration that kept her awake, it was the bewildering events of the entire day. From the moment she met him at the airport to when she got into bed, stripped naked at his instruction, because he wanted 'access to her gorgeous body without impediment'. He had told her that she was a 'object of living art', a canvass upon which he could create...

Having sex for the first time in such a rough and degrading way. Losing her virginity to a man so much older than herself. The paradoxical feelings of being intensely desired and being unfeelingly used at the same time. And the humiliation and exhilaration in the jazz club, leaving her dizzy and uncertain about what she wanted and who she really was. She felt just like a little bird in a storm, not knowing which way was up or down, nor what direction to home and safety... wherever that was.

He had told her that she was to sleep in her room and be available to him there. Never to enter his room unless explicitly told to. There was no key to lock her door and he told her to always leave it open. How could he be so unfair, so demanding, so one-sided? But she hadn't questioned him, just nodded her acquiescence.

The way he was, like Jekyll and Hyde. One moment so caring and kind and the next so cruel and violent. What made him like that? Was it her that brought out the beast in him, or was he just like Mr Hyde? The side that scared her, hurt her, humiliated her. But also aroused her and made her feel intensely desired. Like he would risk everything to be with her.

Or was she the one that brought out the loving Dr Jekyll. The one that spoiled her, guided her, soothed her and made her feel so sexy and grown up. Was it that she liked them both, the combination together making her feel so alive, so carefree, so invigorated? She felt she could be anything when she was with him, because he made her feel safe and secure. He would look after her and tell her what to do.

Despite the craziness of the ordeal, she thought it would be exciting to be here with him for a couple of days and then she would go home to her mundane life and her mother.

Her mother; tired, busy, distracted. Often drinking too much late at night, to numb her perpetual feelings of quiet desperation. Like she had been ever since daddy had died five years before in that horrendous accident, leaving them destitute and alone. No relatives nearby to help, few friends and no support systems. Mum had to work two jobs to make ends meet, so she was never home. Leaving her daughter to cook and clean, do the grocery shopping and the laundry, while trying to keep up at school. Knowing that education was the way out of all of this, but not knowing how she would afford to study after high school.

The loneliness and despair making her vulnerable, needing affection, needing attention, needing appreciation, needing affirmation. Wanting to please others, in the hopes that they give her a bit of what she wanted, so desperately needed. The irony of having to be adult, while not having an emotional foundation of self-awareness nor self-confidence, left her exposed to him.

It was this combination of innocence, immaturity, vulnerability and desire that had captured his imagination when he first started messaging her. He realised he could mould her, make her his, body and soul. With just the right incentives, giving her what she needed, praising her obedience and censuring her if she didn't cooperate. Threatening to take it all away if she resisted.

His own mother had done the same to him, making him achieve her expectations of professional and material success. Praising and spoiling him when he achieved, but becoming angry, cold and distant when he failed. He soon learned that he had to be single-minded and selfish about achieving success, if he was to obtain the affirmation he needed.

This psychopathic focus meant that he was not able to maintain regular relationships built on sharing and intimacy, needing rather to control and dominate. Like he controlled and dominated everything in his life and work. Over time this led him to want to hurt his partner, not severely or sadistically, but for them prove their submission to him and his control over every aspect of their sexuality. This was always followed by the desire to heal and care for the one he had hurt, so that she would be bonded to him and ready for the next round of passion.

Through this journey he developed a fascination with the psychology of seduction and control, the defiling of innocence and the inevitability of a cycle of temptation and succumbing followed by guilt and redemption. The internal conflict that this brings was his foundation of fantasy and reality.

Over the past year he had introduced her to stories of non-consensual and rough sex, registering her on selected internet sites that carried the content he wanted her to know. At first, she was horrified, asking why anyone would want to hurt someone or be hurt.

But over time, he gently explained that in fantasy, anything was acceptable and that many people shared these dark thoughts. He increasingly encouraged her to masturbate while he read an erotic story aloud, ensuring its subconscious connection with her arousal.

The first time she refused, he told her he was going away for a few days and would not be able to talk to her. And maybe she wasn't as grown up as he though she was. After a week of silence, she missed him and craved his attention so much. Learning her lesson, she volunteered to do what he wanted, when he eventually sent her a brief message saying that he was going to be back soon, and did she want to chat.

It wasn't long thereafter that he made her attach clothes pegs to her nipples while she masturbated to him reading. And soon after that, she would pinch her clit painfully to delay her orgasm, while she frigged herself and read the stories aloud to him. At those times, he was quiet, not talking, just watching, while she performed, not even knowing if he was still there, but not stopping until she orgasmed for him, because that is what he had told her to do.

It was with that recollection that she eventually fell into a fitful sleep, not knowing what the next morning would bring.

She woke up, sunlight filtering through the drapes and smells of cooking wafting through the house. In the morning light, and with some sleep, the fear and confusion of the previous night was largely allayed.

When she sat up, she saw that her bag was gone and there was a white bikini laid out at the end of the bed. She was sure there was an explanation about the bag. But it was clear what he expected, so she obeyed and slipped it on.

CHAPTER 8

The bottom was a Brazilian cut, leaving half her ass cheeks exposed as it fitted tightly up her crack, while the top was a couple of triangles with some string, to partly cover her petite breasts, but still making her feel exposed.

She would never have bought something so tiny and revealing by herself, especially to wear in public. Despite this and the feeling that it was definitely a size too small, she realised that she looked pretty sexy. She took a deep breath, swallowed hard to control the butterflies fluttering round her stomach, and sashayed into the kitchen to get his attention.

He was at the stove making scrambled eggs, a pitcher of orange juice besides him, but finishing a large cup of coffee that he didn't offer her. He glanced over his shoulder as she walked in, and then a double take "You look good enough to eat. You're gorgeous. I love the bikini. Come here!"

Grabbing her shoulders in his strong hands, so firm that it almost hurt. Looking her up and down, his face softening into a sensual expression, devouring her as he slipped a hand down her back to caress her ass as he leant in to kiss her gently on the lips. His hand trailed over the bikini onto the exposed skin and down to the crease where her cheek met her thigh, causing a nervous involuntary twitch of her muscles. He slid the sport calloused tip of his index finger softly back and forth, stroking her as delicately as a feather.

"The most erotic part of a woman." He whispered, leaning into her ear so the breath of his voice tickled her lobe, sending sensual tremors down her neck. And then leaning away to continue cooking, leaving her in emotional turmoil. Wanting to be touched but fearing the consequences...

Plating the eggs and pouring the juice he announced. "After breakfast, we're going surfing."

"I don't know how to surf. I'll watch you." Concern on her face, thinking about wearing this bikini in the waves.

"No! I'll teach you. It's easy." With a relaxed smile, but a look that broached no further resistance.

"Please can I change into a different bathing suit? This one's too small." At least that would be better. "I couldn't find my suitcase. Do you know where it is? I have a one-piece swimmers that I could wear."

"NO! You'll wear what I tell you to wear, young lady. I like that one." A hard edge to his voice. "Last night, you wore panties from your case. Without permission. So, I've taken your clothes. I bought you pretty things to wear and I'll choose what's appropriate for each occasion." A clench of his jaw and then. "That's enough. Have your eggs, so we can get to the beach."

A few sullen mouthfuls and gulps of juice later, he told her that if she wanted the bathroom, now was the time. But she didn't need to go, so he whisked her down to the beach, holding her hand securely. Sitting near a couple of cute boys her age, who were chatting and watching the surfers. But distracted now that she was there, whispering and nudging each other, pretending not be watching, but obviously ogling her displayed charms.

"I'll go out first. The waves are a little big right now, but you'll get a chance later." In command of his beach and his life. She a lamb to the slaughter. "But first I'll rub some lotion onto your back. You don't want to get burned."

Lying her down on the towel, first on her stomach, rubbing the lotion over her back and down to her butt. Then up her legs, pushing them apart so he could flick a finger along the exposed thin white band between her thighs, just besides her labia. She felt them begin to squelch with the almost attention of the past 24 hours, the moisture building and a wet spot appearing on the gusset pressed tight to her crotch.

But he pretended not to notice the translucent patch, nor the opportunity, preferring to tell her to make sure she covered her front. As she did, he waxed his longboard. She giggled at the innuendo of him rubbing pineapple fragranced 'Mr Zoggs Sex Wax' onto his board and then jokingly on the front of his boardshorts, while repeating the by-line "The best for your stick" in a creepy voice.

He finished by leaning over and stroking the wax against the translucent spot on her bikini between her legs saying "Later!", causing her to blush as she realised how transparent it was and how obvious he had been in front of those boys.

He winked and then paddled out, while she lay tanning in the Factor 10 that he had intentionally chosen for her fair and sensitive skin. The boys glancing surreptitiously at her gave her a thrill, being so obviously desired.

Watching him surf got her juices flowing again, this man that could do things she had never dreamed of. She realised he owned the waves, like he owned her. And then he was besides her again, telling her it was time for her to learn to surf.

"I can't. I don't know how.' She protested. "I really need to go and pee."

"You'll do as I say, little one." He growled so menacingly that she nearly pee'd herself right there on the beach. "You can go in the sea." As if that was a compromise, a normal thing to do. She had heard her school mates giggling and talking about weeing in the pool but thought that was gross. She would never do that herself, in public. No!

He grabbed her tightly by the hand, and resolutely marched her down to the water. Countenancing no resistance. Wading into the sea, waves hitting her legs and splashing her bikini. Making it totally see-through. She cringed with embarrassment, trying to get deeper in, so the water would cover her displayed pussy from the leering boys on the beach.

"You'd better pee now, because I'm going to push you onto a wave soon." Like he was telling her to go to the bathroom before the show in a movie theatre. She couldn't, wouldn't. Not in public. Not into her bikini. Eeeew. Gross.

He picked her up onto the long surfboard, a powerful hand between her legs, gripping her thigh but pushing firmly up against her crotch, while his other grabbed the board up front, thumb extended distractingly under her breast. And then he pushed her as the wave came and she was thrust forwards with the momentum of nature. She had never felt such power, such exhilaration as time seemed to stand still and she rushed forwards ahead of the wave. Until she fell and it was the opposite. Rolling around in a washing machine, seawater and sand up her nose, in her hair, bashed onto the sand bottom, grazing her shoulder. She surfaced like a wet puppy, bewildered, disoriented, sore. One breast had popped out of her top and was exposed for a couple of seconds, flashing those boys. They definitely saw, because they were ogling her and talking excitedly. But even when she covered up, the bikini was transparent and her nipples were obvious, hard as stones from the cold and something else...

Then he was there, holding her, laughing, making it better. Maybe it wasn't so bad. She could try again at his urging. But now the need to pee was even greater, so she did. Through her bikini bottoms. With the world watching her. She was sure those boys knew what she was doing. She flushed with shame, but at the same time felt a tingle of excitement down between her legs. Was she such a slut that she got off on something so gross?

He dragged her out for the next ride, telling her she must stand. She would have to carry on until she stood on the board, like a real surfer. No lying down and taking the wave. So, she tried and fell. Again, the elation of the surge, followed by the anguish of the fall. More sand, grazes and exposure as her bikini wouldn't stay on.

CHAPTER 9

The sand feeling rough on her sensitive skin as a slight sunburn had turned her pink.

Until eventually she stood, exposing her transparent bikini to the beach and the enthralled boys, who only had eyes for her in the small shore break, not their heroes out on the big waves at backline. He came up to her, hugging her and congratulating her. Telling her how amazing she was to carry on trying, a true champion.

Those words made it worth all the pain and hardship of the previous hours. But now as she walked up the beach, she felt the sand in her bikini, scratching her nipples and abrading her labia. So, distracting that she hardly noticed the huge eyes and grins of the boys as she went past them exhibiting her darkened nipples and swollen pussy lips through the transparent material.

"Did you see her pussy, dude." One boy whispering to the other, voice loud with excitement.

"That's no way to talk in front of a girl." He stood over them, grim expression. "Tell her you're sorry."

"Sorry." The boy mumbled with a red face, not looking at her. She wanted to hide in the sand. Him making a thing of it, was worse than the comment. And then as he smiled and winked at her, she knew he knew that. He had done it on purpose, to embarrass her even more. Tears of frustration threatened to spill from her eyes, as her juices threatened to spill from her crotch.

"Please can I shower." As they went through the villa gate. "I've got sand everywhere."

"Stop being so self-centred. Look what you've done to me." He snarled into her ear, grabbing her hair and indicating the bulge in his boardshorts. Pushing her brusquely to her knees, right there behind the fence. Pulling his shorts down to expose his rampant manhood, bigger and harder than it was the previous night. Dragging her mouth onto it, opening in surprise and resignation, until it was lodged deep and she was instinctively sucking and swallowing the way he had taught her all those times with the dildo on chat.

Her knees started hurting, pieces of course sand pressing against them on the paving, digging into the flesh and bone. The next-door windows gazed accusingly down at her, despite the absence of life. Hoping they're not home, she sucked diligently, her pussy uncomfortable, bikini filled with sand. Him looking pleased with himself as he enjoyed her careful ministrations.

After a while he wanted more and hauled her abruptly up by the arm, turning her to face the sea. A large hand encircling her neck, pushing her over, bent at the waist, legs straight and spread, bikini bottoms ripped down and stretched tight between her knees, making her feel even more naked and vulnerable than if they were off. He enjoyed seeing the flush of her skin where the sun had brightened her back and thighs, contrasting nicely with the ivory where her bikini had covered.

Her hands on the fence for support, so she could see the boys glancing back up at her. Even though she knew they could only see her head, she was certain they knew what was happening. Especially as her mouth opened into a shocked gasping O as he thrust up into her, dragging the sand into her silky depths, scratching her on the inside. "Please don't, it hurts. It's scraping me."

Looking down irritated, he slapped her sun-reddened thigh hard causing stinging pain to shoot up her leg and her head to whip around in shock, accusing eyes looking back at him.

"What did I say yesterday?" Another stinging slap. "About saying no to me!" A third for good measure. Her sun burned thigh now on fire.

"I... I... I should n-n-never say n-n-no?" Her eyes no longer accusing, just accepting and meek, bordering on tears. Preferring the scraping to that terrible sting of his hand.

"So, what do you want me to do?" Embedding the lesson into her consciousness. Staying still, hand holding her hair, cock pinning her tight depths with the grains of sand reminding them both of her earlier defiance.

"Please do what you want." Submissive. Body, heart and soul hurting, evident in her eyes as she looked back at him over her shoulder.

"Do what?" He growled, with pent up lust, still not moving.

"Please fuck me like you want. However you want." Complete capitulation. Looking forward, back to the boys on the beach. Still watching her, whispering to each other. The shame flooding her face with blood to match her sun-burned back.

He started pounding into her like a man possessed, his member feeling like sandpaper scraping against the sensitive skin on her vaginal walls. She could find no pleasure in this act, rather accepting and hoping he would finish soon. But that didn't stop her natural lubrication at the stimulation, making his slide easier and the scratching more intense on her heightened sensitivity. Even as he popped her breast out of the top, the sand scratched her sensitive tit flesh, causing more discomfort.

He also felt the agony, although not as sore. It merely making him last longer, a simple diversion, even if the idea that she was standing there bent over suffering for him, made him harder and more aroused than ever. Riding her, hand bunched in her hair as she pushed back and tightened on his shaft, aiming to make him climax swiftly.

Once he did cum, purposefully jetting his sperm just inside her opening so it would run out as she walked, he pulled her bikini back up, rubbing their fluids up against her vulva, leaving it wet and tart with sand particles sprinkled about her crotch. Nevertheless she had not been able to quench that unending need, even with his pounding her quickly and hard. The gritty squelch of her pussy a continual tactile reminder of her situation.

As they approached the villa. "Strip. Then rinse the sand and everything off before we walk inside."

She knew not to argue. The shower was chilly yet pleasant. Soothing on her sun baked skin, taking the sand off. Then on his command, inserting a finger up inside herself to scoop up cum and sand, cleansing her intimate yet soiled channel. Another another humiliation in a long succession of embarrassing deeds executed on his direction, as he reclined watching, and enigmatic smile flickering across his lips.

"Come come and clean me off of your filth." Once she was clean. At first not knowing what he was saying and then terrified watching him open his board shorts and take his sticky sand peppered organ out for her attention. Sitting down on the edge of his recliner, hesitantly tasting the sour gritty substance. Then swallowing it as he gave her a warning growl as she was ready to spit the disgusting combination out. Felt so little and useless against his relentless expectations.

He started becoming erect with the stimulation making her hopeful she could soon be fulfilled. Guiding her on, before lowering her head and destroying her burning hope, by adding "I'm fatigued, let's go inside to rest."

Dozing on the couch in the lounge, head on his muscled shoulder, body moulded to him, feeling more and more aroused with his male domination and her feminine frustration. Wishing to enquire, yet being too bashful, too hesitant. Him constantly taking the lead, her following. Not sure if she dare ask for freedom, or even how to. So, she lay there twitching, frantic, while he snored lightly, indifferent.

CHAPTER 10

He woke to her fingers going over the thick hairs on his chest, salt and pepper contrasting with his smooth tanned skin. She had been lying on his sleeping form, head resting on his wide chest, listening to his steady strong heartbeat, smelling the male aroma of musky sandalwood from his deodorant combine with the fresh perfume of sea, salt and sun. Those same hairs that she was fiddling with had tickled her nose and excited her nipple, but she wouldn't move for anything.

Despite everything, she felt protected here with his arm unintentionally encircling her, hand placed on her bare hip. This man who had educated her, lavished her, seduced her, made her feel desired and valued like no one else. She was magnetically pulled to him and his power, yielding her control to him, gladly since the intensity of that emotion was like nothing else she had ever felt.

Indeed, he had raped her, harmed her, humiliated her, but then cared for her and repaired her more than her mother, more than anybody else. The day she scraped her knee badly, tumbling after some bullying girls at school had shoved her about, mocking her relentlessly about the way she looked and how geeky she was, always reading, always studying. It was him who taught her that day, before her mother was even home, how to clean it, treat it, bandage it.

All the while praising her how courageous she was, how gorgeous she was, how brilliant, how well-read, how much better she was than those females. Making the agony on her knee and in her heart go away, just that little bit, enough to feel better. Yeah, he told her she had to 'suck it up', not get caught on the agony, but it was all about her, no one else.

Her mother not really engaging her about it, just giving a throw away remark about 'girls-will-be-girls' and she shouldn't take it too seriously. Later that night, he advised her to love and appreciate her mother, but know that she had limited time for a daughter. Telling her that he was here for her, always. Her father figure, not to replace her father but to be present now that he was not.

"What are you doing?" Awakening and peering down at her over the end of his nose, hand slipping down to rub her rear.

"I enjoy resting here on you." Feeling bad, but hoped he understood. "That feels fantastic."

A spark of passion crossed his countenance. His hand now in her hair, tugging it back to bend her neck, lips wide, staring up into his piercing blue-grey eyes, the colour of the sea. His mouth crushing hers, drawing her to him by just her hair, quick jabs of agony as though it's being torn out by the roots. But also, so strong and domineering, his tongue thrusting into her mouth, twisting with her smaller tongue, raging across her little teeth and pink gums, lips pressing each other, teeth occasionally clattering with the ferocity of his kiss. Her delicate sensitive girlish chin stroked and scratched by his day-old harsh stubble. Totally at his mercy.

Her body feels a torrent of emotions as her desire ramps, nipples stiffen to little stones, blush travels over her chest up her neck, stomach quivers deep with small shockwaves, vagina gushes longing for some attention. Doing what it is naturally supposed to do and what he has educated it to do; respond to his command, his attention, his need, his strong muscles crushing her pliant skin.

She feels his manhood probing, hard with eagerness, passion taking over. Rolling onto her with knees widening her legs, the feel of his leathery skin on her silken thighs, his cock turgid and hard prodding at her loins. He guides the head up and down her slit, his smooth glans slipping past her juice-moistened lips, before with one of the powerful thrusts she has learned to expect, he is entrenched in her gripping depths. The suddenness generating a tinge of agony, but making her feel full, entire, complete. His pelvis grinding hard into hers, her clit inflamed and squished, sending shocks through her body, in sync with the pulsating ecstasy from deep in her sex.

He takes her then, balanced on his hands, buttocks rippling as he drives home, her legs spread and looped over his back, heels tapping him hard, forcing him in further. She grabs his chest, not able to reach behind, hands scrabbling vainly like a climber attempting to find a foothold on a rough rock wall, her tiny fingers scraping, leaving nail scars down his sides. Her scorched back rubs on the couch, tingling, itching, hurting the fragile skin, heightening her tactile awareness and the intensity of her experience.

He doesn't seem to notice, only pounds harder. Suddenly a hand around her neck, increasing the pressure, scrutinising her like an eagle clutching its prey. She feels the blood pound in her carotid artery, striving to get to her brain, beyond his tightening fingers. Her hands now clawing at his wrist, in an attempt to halt the gradual wash of blood over her eyes, the creeping blackness, her awareness vanishing, even though he continues to pound her to unconsciousness.

As she faints, he relieves the pressure, so she revives after a couple of seconds. Eyes open, looking for explanations, brief forgetfulness, but then she feels the cock enter her, assaulting her depths with little regard beyond its own fulfilment. Her body responding, whether conscious or unconscious; lubricating, stimulating, arousal peaking.

An intriguing smirk passes over his lips as he starts squeezing again and she starts struggling. This time her whole body, writhing against the oncoming blackness, making the sensation that more greater for the predator inside him. Enjoying the fact that he controls everything, even while she is aware. At his whim. Yet despite of her resistance, he pushes her to another blackout and her pussy to even greater wetness as the fear endorphins race through her veins.

Coming around again, she says without air 'Stop! Please?" And at the same time her hips buck automatically into his, attempting to bring him deeper, pushing her up towards her impending summit. And without a trace of compassion, he merely repeats the pressure on her neck a third time. His own blood boils, the sensations of her shaking body, her clenched cunt, her frantic gaze, her ragged breath, her sweat-soaked skin propelling him ahead.

Emerging from the silent darkness, this time all she can feel is the heat in her loins as it accepts his firm, sleek organ. Delicate skin sinking into delicate folds, moistened by her moisture and his precum, sliding ecstatically, making him cum, deep powerful jets of his seed, washing her womb, filling her with a warmth that sets off the orgasm she has been craving for since the previous night.

"Clean me off." When he rises up, seemingly undisturbed by the crescendo of sensations she was sure he must have felt. Her body still resonating with the shocks and bliss of her climax. Obediently sucking and licking their secretions off his wilting manhood, feeling their fluids drip out of her own fulfilled but defiled hole, her feelings neglected while his are fed. Humiliated at the contrast, she merely stares down at the task she is doing, unable to meet his eyes, her surrender absolute.

"I promised you three ear piercings." The transition to transactional, perplexing her, appearing blank. "Well, come now. Certainly you recall. A month ago, you claimed you wanted piercings and your mother had forbade it." Now nodding with recall. "I said I'd organise it, but there was something you needed do first."

"Thank you. Yes. I desperately want three studs here. It'd be so kewl." The naïve girl, touching the upper portion of her left ear, as she was already visualising the studs.

CHAPTER 11

"We'll go this afternoon. But first your half of the contract." He proceeded into the kitchen returning with a tiny bowl and a tin box.

"Lay down. We're going to place this in your left tit. To match your earrings." Holding out a slender half-inch gold ring, as he placed the bowl and tin on the side table.

She gazed at him in bewilderment. "I don't want it. . ."

He rushed so rapidly that he had gripped her by the throat again, with a ruthless hold, before she understood what was happening. Her hands moved up to his wrist to lessen the strain, as he whacked her left breast, extremely hard, leaving a crimson handprint blossoming on the precious white flesh, blending with the red sunburn surrounding the little pale triangle imprinted by her bikini top.

She screamed and grasped her breast as the hot stinging sensation struck her head. His palm returning, backhand onto the right breast, indenting and then wavering as another bruised red mark developed. She started crying and gripping her agonised chest, staring up at him as if he were a monster.

"Put. Your. Fucking. Hands. Down. NOW!" Rage pouring from his countenance looking at her tear-filled eyes. Her hands fell, replaced by his. Twisting a nipple and asking. "Whose tits are these?"

Complete knowledge of the circumstance she was in filled her face. She said slowly, not meaning it, but knowing it was the only response in that moment "Y-y-yours?"

"Well, if I want to slap them, what do you do?" Almost friendly in his tone. Bewilderment by the tremendous contrast from seconds before.

"I let you?" Every particle of her existence resisted the assertion, yet her intellect couldn't imagine denying him the truth.

In any event, it didn't help, since he whacked her left breast again.

"That's right. And if I want to put rings in them, what do you do?"

"I... I... l-l-let y-y-you." Sobbing in defeat.

"See, you can learn. With a little discipline." He grinned, even his eyes crinkling. "Let's try again. Lay down. I'm going to puncture your nipple. What do you say?"

"Ok. . . alright. . . Th-thank you?" Again, not sure how he wanted her to answer, but trying to ease his fury. She could cope with this. That wouldn't be too horrible. And then she could take it out when she got home. At least she would have the studs in her ears. She wouldn't take those out, because she'd undoubtedly have earned them.

He swabbed her nipple with spirit alcohol, making it stand erect from the cold. She was on her back on the sofa hands below her backside so that they wouldn't move. He enjoyed the way the nip puckered, stiffened by the draining alcohol chilling the skin. And he was convinced, the dread he saw in her eyes was adding, while the excitement of their fucking was likely to be fading.

Her little areolae were reacting in anticipated ways. Pink skin crinkling, glands rising as though in wrath, the hue darker as blood raced to the cooling flesh. He flicked the nub and squeezed the nipple region to ensure they stayed stiff and erect for the impending needle.

Her face pinched with anxiety, her lips puckered into a tight rosebud of misery. She'd automatically bent her shoulders as if it would minimise the ache that she was afraid would drive her mad. Her entire existence protested at the notion of his piercing her breast, yet there was no way out. Not with this dude.

Not able to gaze as he took two chunks of ice and clamped the terribly erect nipple between them tight, scorching her with the cold and pressure. The freeze turned her nipple light pink-blue, forcing the blood away, making the nubs firmer, more erect, like hard pencil erasers protruding out of the rising mounds of her delicate breasts. The chilly anguish lancing her body like she thought the coming needle would.

She clenched her teeth when he reached over to fetch the tool of her agony. Involuntarily peering down, she realised he held a big sewing needle between his thumb and fingers. He brought it to the outside of her nub, while pressing her breast flesh tightly to make the nipple pop up and stand proud.

Blood surged in and she saw her rock-hard nipple involuntarily meet the incoming onslaught of the needle, keeping firm so the undesired steel could enter its depths, forever ruining and harming her lovely breasts. He circled the needle as if attempting to choose the ideal position, but was merely waiting for the nipple to rewarm after the ice, so the impact would be that much more noticeable. The scrapes on her sensitive skin stung while she waited, observing. He prolonged the process out, so the anticipation was more torturous than the deed, each nick of her breast like a wound deep into her heart. Her teat prickled with excitement and heightened sensitivity, as the warmth returned.

"Don't move." Gradually, he pressed the needle into the crinkled skin, feeling its sponginess give way before the tip started to break through. "Keep motionless else it'll slash your breast." How could he say that so calmly? Such an awful thing to say. What a dreadful thought. How would she stay motionless with this pain? Forced on her by the man who professed to want to protect her.

"Pleeeeeeeeaaaaaaaasssssseeeee." That was really painful. "Stooooooooop." Gritting her teeth, fearing his mutilating her treasured breast, she clinched her hands and lay wilfully motionless. Her toes curled, her legs tight. Gorgeous face in a rictus of misery, but he didn't see. He just had eyes for the needle, burrowing into her tight nipple.

He steadily pushed the needle through the elastic skin until it speared out the other side with a single drop of blood, and then another. It streamed crimson down the side of her breast like the clear tears were streaming down the side of her face. The agony, the blood, the moment, overpowered her and she collapsed as previously, but not because he did it physically, but because the mental anguish of the encounter became too great. But he was not happy to let her depart and waited until she recovered consciousness a few of minutes later, peering up at him like a scared mouse about to be devoured by a vicious predator.

He then wriggled and twisted the needle, forcing her breast up into a cone, firing daggers of pain into her chest. A short dab of the spirits to disinfect, before replacing needle with the ring, which he clasped closed.

Bending down and first kissing the pierced nipple before sucking the blood off her breast and the tears from her face he muttered, "See that wasn't so horrible, was it?"

She couldn't answer. Laying there, the blazing anguish becoming a dull ache, realising that her body had been desecrated. But with her agreement, even if it had been wrung from her under fear. She had participated and not resisted. Was there a tiny part of her that desired this, ached for it, like she sought his attention and intimacy. The feelings were all too much and her brain too young to understand it all, to cope with the complexity of emotions he had released in her psyche.

"You also wanted a belly-button ring, if I recall properly." He said pleasantly. "We'll also receive that today. But in exchange, I want to put this in your other nipple." Picking up a similar nipple ring, followed by her screams of anguish.

The sign over the business door said 'Jimmy's Studs and Tats'. After suffering two home piercings, she was less keen to continue through with her prior wish, but he had brought her here nevertheless, explaining cryptically "A promise is a promise."

CHAPTER 12

It was not apparent to her whether it was his commitment to her or vice versa, that led in her hesitantly entering the piercing and tattoo shop.

When her second delicate nub had been so mercilessly punctured, he had complemented her about how lovely they were and how courageous she had been, all the while holding her and caressing her hair, as she screamed out her anguish and sadness. She gently melted into him, recovering her composure, despite the constant stinging reminder at the points of her breasts.

He cajoled her into dressing in a gorgeous Indian cotton floral sundress with wedge sandals, making her appear just like any other late-teen, even though she thought she had little in common with most other girls her age. This time, he allowed her wear a little tight white thong but no bra, which pleased her since she didn't want anything irritating her sensitive nips. She was happy to discover that the rings didn't show through the loose cotton, but she couldn't get used to the fact that they kept her nipples perpetually erect and aroused by the continual stimulation and throbbing.

When she had first seen him, she had dressed pretty dowdily, almost tom-boyish, hoping not to be noticed by anybody. She liked to avoid intimate relationships with other people, to focus on her life's love, which was reading books. Or rather literature, as she termed it with all the seriousness that a teenager could manage. Most of her connections were relatively anonymous internet conversations, where she felt sheltered from the hazards that actual interactions brought.

Over time, he had urged her to dress more female, more grownup, in tighter clothing that revealed more leg or flesh. He pushed her to buy online, using the money he deposited onto the e-wallet, but only after he had approved of them.

A year previously, she would never have been caught dead in a short sundress that displayed her slender legs, arms and shoulders. Yet she had slipped it on without thinking, as she had the seductive underwear that had replaced the practical panties that she used to wear. There too was a long-term process of grooming, urging her to look like a lady, showing her photographs of attractive ladies in exposing erotic lingerie to desensitise her. It wasn't long until she gladly did modelling presentations for him, wearing her most recent items and toying with herself for his enjoyment.

At the beginning, all he had done was convey suggested suggestions that she should dress differently. She attempted to encourage her mother to buy clothes she imagined he may appreciate but was constantly nervous that her selections wouldn't suit him. Her mother typically wouldn't readily afford or agree to the things she desired, so she lived in perpetual fear of his displeasure.

Then he couriered the smartphone with e-wallet and assured her she could buy stuff independently, without her mother knowing. At first, she was pleased, since she could decide. But after a few poor choices, that he urged her to return since they did nothing for her, she was distraught and started seeking his approval for her picks of underwear and even everyday clothing. Gradually, he began indicating what she should buy, what she should wear and how she should wear it, taking the options away from her and hence the fear of 'doing it wrong'.

In this process, he pushed her away from the types of fashionable outfits teens were wearing towards more mature dress. Neither trashy or exposing but clothing that men rather than teens would love. She assumed the more sensual sophisticated look of a confident twenty-something-year old that turned men's minds, particularly when paired with the fresh innocent face, clumsiness and naivety of an eighteen-year-old girl. Even her subtly exquisite cosmetics couldn't cover her youthfulness while her movements exposed her lack of expertise.

Being just five-foot-tall, he put her into heels, initially little inch-high Rose Clara's, but eventually to three-inch sandals once she could walk firmly in them. She felt the pressure of her toes, the tightness in her calves and the roll of her bottom when she wore heels, but the height it provided her made it worth it. Especially when he complemented her and told her how gorgeous she looked. At first, she kept her new clothing from her mother, but with time she understood that her mother was just too busy and self-absorbed in her own unhappiness to actually notice and only sometimes condemned her ensembles. Her mother really sounded relieved when she claimed she was purchasing them with the money she made waitressing at the neighbourhood pizza business.

Therefore, she proceeded to wear what she wanted, when she wanted. Or rather, what he desired.

Her mother's apathy was in sharp contrast to the encouragement and comments he offered her when she showed him what she was wearing, whether video chat, WhatsApp or SnapChat. Finally he persuaded her to email him images and gifs of herself every day, mostly innocent but some explicit ones, up her skirt or down her cleavage.

The most embarrassing was when he instructed her to go out sans underpants and email him proof. Capturing and emailing images of her nude pussy or exposed breasts made her flush with embarrassment, even when no one was looking. Yet without fail, the images plainly revealed how horny it made her, dampness adhering to her pussy lips or nipples standing proudly at attention, just for him.

She found herself the centre of guys wherever she went, strolling on the street, working at the pizza business, shopping at the grocery store, observing her with glances she had not encountered before. A hunger and an intensity that she found weird and unpleasant yet made her pussy throb with delight and her nipples tighten into little pebbles, lovingly enveloped by her lovely new underwear.

But rather than being ignored as she tried to reach the top shelf for groceries, there was always a man there to help her, beaming down with a fire in his eyes. Elderly guys now let her into the checkout queue in front of them, seeking to make small chat with her.

CHAPTER 13

Whenever she lost an item, it wasn't her who leapt to pick it up, it was the males who always appeared to be close in the aisle.

She started seeing guys gazing covertly, even guiltily, as she sashayed down the street and could feel the attention of those following her, ogling her rolling hips and slim legs. When she informed him about it, he stated that it was because she was a beautiful seductive lady and that guys desired her. Not to worry, but to exploit her femininity to her advantage.

Earlier, she was invisible to everyone, but progressively a couple of her male professors showed her greater attention. She was particularly happy when her English instructor, began to comment more favourably on her work.

Her gratuities also started growing from serving pizza, particularly from groups of guys who looked to be undressing her with their gaze and attempting to see down her top, when she stooped over to offer them their food or beverages. She learnt how to maximise those tips, with a delicate movement of her breast, lick of her lips or twitch of her butt when she knew they were looking.

This reinforced her notion that the way he was clothing her was to help her be more grownup and more confident, so she continued to welcome his creeping control over her life.

Before she had a profile handle that was pretty youthful and girlish, but he started referring to her as 'my little Dove' in their conversations, in allusion to a bird he was teaching to fly. He never used her given name and finally got her to alter her handle to @Littlepet, only ever calling her Dove. This was also the name he chose for her phoney ID, so that while she was with him, she always felt like an innocent bird confronting the tumult of the world but knowing that she could return to his protected clutches. He had promised to get her some new books after shopping for some new lovely clothes and underwear that wouldn't bother her nipples. But first she had to receive the promised piercings. With two standard piercings on her earlobe, she wanted to embellish her top left ear helix with three multicoloured studs. While in the chair, it didn't take long for the piercing gun to do its work on the cartilage, like wasp-stings leaving aquamarine, pink and white stones embedded in a row.

She had recovered her old zest and enjoyed her new edgy style, instantly feeling more adult. This made her enthusiastic and ready to undergo the navel piercing. She had to draw up the hem of her dress to enable the piercer, whose nametag read 'Megan', access to her belly button, wondering if that was why he had made her wear a dress and the little thong, rather than a skirt and shirt which would have been lot simpler. The mischievous smirk she detected when gazing towards him as she exposed herself, reinforced her doubts. Yet the urge to get the hard-earned piercing, exceeded the shame of revealing her gorgeous underpants.

Thankfully, they were in a confined room and Megan looked entirely indifferent about anything other than her business, so blushing prettily to herself she laid back with her bottom half exposed. Although she had picked the three ear studs and undergone the piercings, he had selected a gorgeous top-down navel ring with a row of colourful stones.

"I like this. And it complements your three new studs." He passed it to Megan.

Megan noticed. "The ring has a thicker post, so I'll have to use a stronger gauge needle. It'll hurt a bit more and take longer to recover. Are you alright with that?" Chatting to her.

He answered promptly. "That's OK. Isn't it?" Sending her a predatory smile with a severe glare. "We'll just have to take care of it."

"I think. . . That is pretty." Nothing else she could say.

Sharp pain accompanied the piercing, reminding her of her aching nipples, but not drawn out quite as long. And soon she was the happy owner of a bellybutton ring. The thing she couldn't fathom was why all this exposing and piercing made her crotch tingle, in tune with the throbbing of her piercings.

As she took down her dress, she spotted the moist patch on her underwear between her legs. Not sure if it was her erection or his come from earlier, she blushed deep scarlet, particularly because she didn't know whether Megan had seen too. She excused herself and hurried to the restroom to wash herself dry, even going so far as to wipe inside in case there was any goo there. Seeing the clear liquid on the toilet paper convinced her that it was her secretions, Not his that had wet her underwear.

A sensation of mortification fell over her, even though she had just achieved what she had been fantasising about for decades. The repeated juxtaposition of delight and humiliation that she experienced with him, and the way her body and mind responded still baffled the young lady. During the last year she had gotten increasingly used to it and tried to dismiss whatever misery it caused, since if she concentrated on it too long, she grew upset and furious at herself. And at him, which never ended very well. It was easy to merely endure these inconveniences in exchange for the security and attention.

As she came out of the bathroom, he seized her hand forcefully and carried her briskly through the mall to the La Perla store. Unlike many males, he walked in calmly, taking her to some of the sexiest lingerie in the shop. He spent the next five minutes picking a number of matched combinations, talking to himself as much as to her.

"Hmmm. This is sexy. It'll push your adorable little titties up nicely. Give you some cleavage." He was eyeing a skimpy push-up bra and lace high-leg bikini panty combination in turquoise.

"Oh absolutely. I adore this. Your ass will look lovely." Burgundy thong with black trim and a matching front clipped bra.

"Great to highlight your new rings." Black quarter-cup bra that would scarcely cover her nipples with an even more minuscule g string.

Then smiled sweetly to an attendant who had wandered over and inquired if they needed assistance, with a curious look at the imagined father making such provocative words to his daughter.

"No thanks, we're alright. We know what we want."

Blushing and staring down at the floor, not at the next piece he grabbed - a little purple set with a very low-cut cups and high-cut panty. She had gotten accustomed to him picking her sexy lingerie over the last few months. It started with her making the picks, but gradually the decisions shifted to him as he told her some of her selections didn't 'fit her' and she'd have to return them. Developing her obedience to him. It had become simpler and easier just to let him take the lead.

So, that is what she did when he suggested, "Let's go and try them on."

He shamelessly stepped into the changing room with her, disregarding the astonished look on the attendant's face. Thankfully, there were no other customers, so he got his way despite the pathetic attempt of the woman to beg him to leave. He relaxed on a couch in the separate room just outside the curtained changing room, to enjoy her modelling the underwear and provide directions on how to show them off to best effect.

"Turn over and bend down, legs straight, grasp your calves and stare at me." She found herself showing her taught ass with the teal panties crawling up her crack and her breasts slipping out of the bra. She never questioned the request, having been used to showing herself for him at his direction. At least they were alone, the attendant having gone off in a rage when he had refused to leave. Therefore, there were no witnesses to the sensuous farce.

CHAPTER 14

Just thinking about what she must look like in this suggestive stance made her blush scarlet and quiver in ashamed anticipation of what he could want her to do next. The lustful smile on his face warned her it would not be mild. She felt a combination of terror and thrill, conditioned over time via the more risky exhibitionist actions he had had her do online.

But suddenly everything was different. This was real life, without the shelter of her computer. It made it that much more scary and that much more exhilarating, tapping into the suppressed exhibitionist tendency that he had glimpsed the first time she displayed her tits to the public and that he had carefully fostered ever since.

"Come over here and lean towards me." Wearing the black outfit with her nipples and their rings shown enticingly by the shelf bra. As she performed what he asked, he tweaked each nipple and then tugged them gently by the rings, driving jolts of pain through her delicate breasts.

Then taking a grip of her pale breast flesh encircled by the pink sunburn. "We need to get you an all-over tan. These white spots just don't do justice to this gorgeous bra."

When she donned the purple ensemble, he again called her over informing her. "Spread your legs a little bit. . . No wider." His palm went up her thigh to the thin material concealing her pussy, where he slipped a finger beneath the gusset and directly into her hot hole.

"Please don't. Someone could see." She complained, politely attempting to seal her legs against his entering finger.

"Haven't we discussed this already?" He hissed, hooking his finger into her and cruelly squashing her clit with his thumb, catching her attention and making her pussy juice even more, despite the anguish and embarrassment. "You do not say no to me. Not EVER! Now place your foot up here." Indicating the arm of the chair on which he was seated and drawing her towards him by his grasp on her crotch.

She did what he instructed, thinking that the earlier she obeyed the sooner her experience would be done. She could see the attendant, attempting to peep into the fitting room to see what was going, but thankfully his body disguised the finger fucking he was now giving her increasingly sopping twat.

"Lovely! Quick access and sexy as heck." He complimented her.

As she watched the attendant start heading towards them with a determined look, her blood flowed ice cold and her cheeks burned scorching hot. "That woman is coming. . ." Was all she could murmur, begging him with her eyes.

He laughed and removed his finger, slapped her softly on the rear, saying. "Go off then, you little minx. I guess there's one more to try."

She saw that her fluids were splattered over the panty crotch, when she pulled them down, causing her a moment of terror, as she thought that they would have to carry them to the checkout counter for everyone to see. Desperately trying to wipe the offending liquid off on her dress to make it less noticeable, she was distracted by a shouted voice.

"Sir. I absolutely must ask you to wait outside. Males are not permitted in here." The attendant becomes vociferous with her disdain.

"Okay. Let's go, tiny dove. I'll be waiting outside by the stockings. Bring all of the undergarments. These look very fantastic." She could sense the enjoyment in his voice and was convinced he was glaring mockingly at the woman as he said it.

He was where he had said he would be, having selected a couple thigh high stockings in different colours, one of which had a garter belt. She offered him the underwear and blushed as he raised an eyebrow and grinned at the black patch on the purple panties, bringing them to his nose and took a long whiff, all the while gazing her squarely in the eyes.

She couldn't hold his sight, dropping her eyes to her feet, hands clutched anxiously in front of her, like an embarrassed schoolgirl. She thought to herself that no one should have to undergo such anguish, but it did not stop the fluid slickening her wicked pussy. She also couldn't look up as he paid for the item, speaking nonchalantly to the snooty woman about the wonderful lingerie offered in the shop and that they were sure to return again soon.

On their way out, she wanted the floor to open and swallow her whole, when she overheard the woman mumbling "... just a girl. Disgraceful."

CHAPTER 15

Bright and joyful as if nothing unpleasant had happened, he took her hand and exclaimed, "Time to get some books."

It was via her love of books that he had originally taken her under his control. Early on he had detected her neediness and desire to please, leading him to feel that she had submissive traits that he might foster. He offered her care, establishing her trust and encouraging her to speak up about her thoughts and wants.

When inquiring about her favourite courses at school, she said that English literature was her best. There prompted an extended debate about the works she appreciated the most, such as Bram Stoker's 'Dracula' and Clara's Austin's 'Pride and Prejudice'. They explored gothic horror and romance and the roles of men and women represented in both.

This offered him an opportunity to ask her how she regarded the relationship between Dracula and Kelly or Mina. With a little of cautious supervision, she revealed that both girls were controlled by the supernatural power of the Count. In other works, the themes of wild free women giving vent to their passions and loves, in contrast to the monotony of traditional societal duties, resonated with her naïve senses.

He recommended Emily Bronte's 'Wuthering Heights' which produced endless conversations on the nature of fixation around Heathcliff and the various roles of Catherine and Isabella. Thomas Hardy's 'Far from the Madding Crowd' and 'Tess of the d'Urbervilles' maintained this subject of passion driving women's liberation from societal mores to follow a man, often with unanticipated results, but their own 'emancipation'.

After a talk about her fondness of Anne Rice's 'Vampire Chronicles', which she vastly prefered to the 'tacky Twilight series', allowed him to inform her about Anne Rice's BDSM writings, under her nom de plume Anne Rampling. After reading them, she was amazed at how someone would desire such a life. Yet it enabled a long back and forth on the strength of submission and the devotion to a dominant that channelled pain and service into satisfaction and security for the submissive.

She criticised '50 Shades of Grey' as middle age women's erotica, which opened the door to her reading 'The Tale of O'. It was only afterwards in response to her curious scepticism, that he told her it was written by a woman as a series of letters to her boyfriend, illustrating the ideas of a woman enjoying the attraction and indirect power of utter surrender.

It wasn't a major step from there to her reading sexy stories on non-consent and rape sites and found herself thrilled by the concepts. All through this process, he trained her and encouraged her own discoveries, never pushing too hard, but constantly pushing her ahead. And now here they were, she having followed her enthusiasm at his invitation in coming to the island, despite all reasonable considerations and her prenatal instincts advising her not to.

Watching her explore through the shelves of the bookshop, her exquisite slim body emphasised by the sundress, he pondered about that instructive voyage. He basked in the delight he had received in shaping her naïve senses into an acquiescent dependent young lady, pleasantly pleased at how swiftly he had been able to push her boundaries in ways that more mature women wouldn't allow. He grinned softly at the thought of her hidden nipple rings and the future trials he planned to put her through, to finish the process of converting her into his obedient subservient sex-toy.

He bought the books she picked that day, purposely encouraging her freedom to choose, in the hope of her complete submission to him afterwards. Yet it delighted him to find a highly rated dark erotic novel in amongst the usual classics she had picked.

He threw his arm around her shoulder as they walked, bringing her close, towering over her and almost drowning her with his might. On the way out of the mall, he detoured, bringing her into a jewellery store to buy a neck chain that he claimed to have previously picked.

As he wrapped it around her neck the solid gold chain felt cold against her scorched skin and the twisted knotted gold pendant hung heavily on her chest, bringing attention down to the gentle swell her pert mounds. Clasping it closed and softly massaging her shoulders, he whispered in her ear. "This is for being such a courageous girl today. We'll both like it."

She grinned back at him with pride, feeling like a spoilt princess, and chatted pleasantly all the way back to the villa, the agony of her previous piercing and exhibition seemingly forgotten.

On coming, he guided her with a forceful hand on the back of her neck, right into the middle of the lounge, to stand in front of the sofa on which he had previously taken her, mistreated her and ringed her.

"Stand here!"

A quick staccato command issued in a calm forceful tone that anticipated obedience. She couldn't resist a flood of mixed feelings wash over her as he walked to seat on the couch in front of her. The thumping of her heart accelerated with her fear, knowing that he had something planned, but not knowing what. Why else would she be standing before him, as if on a stage?

"Take off your dress."

She glanced at him uncertainly but knew not to protest. He'd seen her naked so many times, this was no different. However his tone had changed, somewhat husky as if overpowered by emotion or want. Looking into his eyes she saw the hunger, the beast inside, the want commanding him.

And she realised that it was she that pulled it out, made him loose control. This powerful guy at the mercy of her womanhood and his passion for her. She almost swooned as a profound sensation of her own attractiveness and femininity washed over her, tremors spreading over her skin, into her yearning nipples and her pouring sex.

When she pulled the hem of her dress, over her little damp panties, up past her flat pierced stomach, revealing her perky ringed boobs, she watched his hunger deepen. She also observed the developing bulge in his pants, when he slipped off his belt and she uncertainly let the dress flutter to the floor besides her. Standing there before him, her delicate female contours shown to his gluttonous gaze, feeling fully and utterly exposed, despite the little panties he had picked for her earlier.

"Kneel here."

His voice harsh, the animal being released. She slid elegantly to her knees between his, shoulders back, bottom on her heels, hands on her thighs. Showing herself, her gorgeous round globes, little white triangles against flushed pink skin. Her silky skin, making him want to touch it, seize it, defile it, but holding back a few minutes longer, to increase the tension.

Her expression a mix of excitement and trepidation, not knowing what he would do next. Yet knowing it would be difficult, challenging, but hopefully fulfilling. Yet her thoughts awhirl with the unknown, apprehension unleashing flutters in her tummy and pounding in her chest. Her slim shoulders, drawn back, skin stretched taught against her bones and muscles, like a flawless mannequin.

"Keep still."

Holding the end of the belt he tapped the inner of her breast, on the white delicate flesh. Not forceful enough to hurt but stunning in its unexpectedness. She cringed away at the sound, the surprise, the sensation of the belt rapping on her fragile orb, swaying with the blow. The shock of him smacking her there, her expression melting into perplexity at this seeming betrayal.

CHAPTER 16

"Doooon't Moooooovel!"

Shoulders back, chest out. Tiny pointed shoulder-blades projecting from her slim back, expressing her determination to comply. Her look was one of anxiety and terror, but she clinched her teeth and waited patiently. Again, he tapped. This time, she stayed still. Against her instinct, against everything her head was telling her. He struck. She kept her post. Again. . . And again. . . And again.

Her skin was turning red and sensitive after the tenth tap, so he turned to the other unaffected side, repeating the rhythmic pounding on her flesh. When it too was inflamed, he flipped back and forth between them, forehand-backhand like he was playing tennis. Never hard, but persistent and repeated.

Suddenly her toes were curling, in fact both her feet were tightening, striving to bear her misery. Her lips pursed in concentration, preventing any sound. The physical agony was horrible, but it was the emotional hurt that she found most difficult. Having to kneel motionless while her boyfriend abused her, for what?

He marvelled at her strength, her obedience, suffering this entirely unneeded anguish for him, not as punishment for any error or misdemeanour, but because he instructed her to. Amazed at her readiness to surrender herself to his will, tolerating her maltreatment, for no apparent purpose other than his delight.

Shocked at how red her tits were growing, he put out his left hand to cup her right orb, lift it and slide his thumb over the redness, between each tap. Captivated by the warmth of her skin and the plaintive expression she gave him as she instinctively pushed her breast forwards into his hand for comfort, hoping that he would cease the unrelenting agony of her delicate orbs.

Most other ladies he had known would give up, in wrath or in tears. Yet she pushed through all of those feelings and took what he provided, simply for him and what she wanted or needed from him. He was curious at how much farther he would be able to push her until she broke, her limits broken.

By around the thirtieth swot on each, it started to really sting. Hunching her shoulders in an attempt to shield her fragile mounds, she peered up at him, eyes weeping, a single tear sliding down her face and onto her trembling lip. She timidly appealed. "Please stop, it's hurting."

"It's intended to." He stated it calmly, with an uncompromising face but a sympathetic grin, despite observing a second and then a third tear dropping from her eye. Without halting the incessant rapping. "I want you to stay motionless, offer your tits and receive it. To express your affection for me, your loyalty to me. Exactly like O!"

With the maelstrom of emotion racing through her young naïve mind, she clutched onto his words, love and dedication. He loved her. He cared. More than anybody had before. That's what mattered most. She could do this for him. She battled every instinct in her little body in order to keep still for him, not to scream out, not to implore for him to stop.

She stretched out her breasts to meet his unrelenting belt, setting her jaw boldly, shoulders back, straining so as not to flinch, fighting to ignore the agony and win his praise, as numerous tears flowed down her cheeks. Her entire mind, everything she was at that moment, was centred on her breasts, the misery the only thing she could think of, or could feel.

Her slender physique strained urgently for his indulgence, her ribs clearly defined on her heaving chest, her back arched provocatively, her tears causing her body to quiver so enticingly that he debated suspending the pounding to move on to the next part. He wanted to grip the fiery flesh to tactilely savour the misery that he saw in her eyes and in her cries. Yet he knew if he stopped, she would resist any more slaps. And he was not yet finished. . .

So, he didn't stop. He had the patience of an experienced manipulator. At the fiftieth hit her flesh was redder than the surrounding sunburn. Silent tears were flowing down her cheeks from her bulging red eyes, yet she managed to keep still for him and accept the torture without complaint.

"Nice girl. I'm really proud of you."

The tension flowed out of her body with his words, as he stopped pounding her. He bent down and, on each breast, he kissed the searing flesh, letting his tongue run slowly towards the nipple which he delicately sucked. He could feel the heat on his lips and amazed at her endurance, her fortitude. During the experience, accepting all he had hurled at her. Yet he was not yet finished. . .

He held her head in his hands, stared into her eyes and kissed the tears off her cheeks, sucking and tasting them sensually, before kissed her forehead and resting his lips on her skin for long minutes. For that minute she felt protected and thought that the strength it needed to suffer for him was worth it. To prove her dedication and gain his affection.

Suddenly, he had a tube of skin lotion and was pouring it into her irritated breasts, stroking them gently with his calloused fingertips. Although relaxing, it chafed the sensitive skin, eliciting a dual pleasure-pain feeling that she serenely bore.

"Don't move."

Her nearly trance was interrupted as he spoke. He took hold of her necklace to hook an open twist through her left nipple ring. It stung as he dragged it across to tie another twist to the other nipple ring, essentially pushing her breasts together to form a crevasse from her cleavage, held up by the chain around her neck like some sort of wicked bra.

"Ouch! It hurts. Please take it off." She raised her hands to extricate herself, but he smacked them down. The combination of her sensitive nipples, her tormented breasts and her tight burnt skin meant her breasts had become a focus of greater agony and suffering, rather than any pleasure.

"Leave it! That's what it's built for."

CHAPTER 17

Realisation flooded across her. He had really bought the jewellery for himself, not for her. So that he might use her own jewelery to torture and demean her. She was horrified at how naïve and foolish she felt, believing it was something unique just for her. But he had stated it was for her being brave and they would both love it. Maybe he meant she might like wearing it and he would enjoy using it like way. That she must be brave now and suffer for him again? To express her love and loyalty.

Taking down his trousers he slid down till his behind was perched on the edge of the chair and his thighs split wide. She glanced aghast at his semi-erect organ, bobbing just in front of her chest.

"Suck me hard. Then leave some spit on it. You're going to fuck me with your tits, therefore you'll need the lubricant." His brief orders had been stated in a terse decisive tone, but with none of the hate oozing from the meaning of those words.

She gazed at him in frozen dread, not being able to fathom what he wanted her to do with her agonised breasts.

"NOW!"

He strengthened his determination by smacking his belt over those exact same breasts. Jerking with the blow, she hurriedly leant forwards to suck his cockhead into her mouth, not desiring to offend him nor receive any more 'inspiration'.

He was erect in a matter of seconds, the sexiness of her slim body bending to service him, hands on her thighs, staring up at him in anguish, his cock deep in her mouth was too much to resist, even if he had wanted to. This mixed with the power he felt at her obedience, ready to hurt herself for his pleasure, offered him the best aphrodisiac for his passion. She felt the unpleasant swelling in her lips, understanding that she would soon have to massage this enormous engorged monster between her delicate painful mounds. She felt nauseous to her stomach with that notion and frustrated with herself at her lack of will to resist.

"It's time. Slide me between your tits." He was smiling encouragingly at her, appreciating her amazing mouth, but seeking her full obedience. Her suffering for his happiness.

She had seen tit-fucking on porn films and understood the essentials, but none of them looked like this, nor felt like this, she was sure. When his cock moved into the narrow gap between her little straining breasts, it simultaneously scraped the delicate flesh, scratched the scorched skin and strained her aching nipples. In all those films, the women had huge ample breasts between which to catch a stiff penis. She merely had little pert mounds that could scarcely squeeze together, much alone produce adequate cushion for his stimulation.

Yet, she stooped her waiflike shoulders and pressed the meagre flesh together from the sides, to lessen the straining of her nubs and the tugging of the chain around her neck. But it merely generated extra friction on her delicate cleavage. The cream eased his cock's passage, but it ached like hell and she was having to do all the effort herself, while he reclined blissfully watching her with amused curiosity and that dark hunger shining in his eyes.

Yet, it didn't stop her from pressing down and pulling up to jerk him off, hurting herself again and over again, generating shouts of delight from him and sobs of anguish from her. She moved her fingers across the front of her sore orbs, so she could gently clasp her nipples between her fingers in an attempt to alleviate the pain while she rode him with her chest.

"You'll have to move a bit quicker if you want me to cum. That's the only way to finish." His pleasant voice belying the violent meaning of his remarks. "I know it seems challenging, but you must learn to focus on satisfying me. Not on yourself." Observing her closely while she listened, but without meeting his eyes nor recognising his demand. "Look at me. Do you understand?" A hesitant nod, with concerned eyes elevated to his unsympathetic face. "Then get on with it."

She started again, squeezing her agonised tits over his turgid shaft, her lips pursed, her brow screwed in concentration, new tears flowing down her cheeks, accumulating on the point of her chin. Then flowing onto her breasts, adding insignificantly to the lubricant that wasn't facilitating the passage of his manhood between her sensitive breasts.

He was both astonished and completely satisfied by how far he had been able to drive her. He couldn't get over the notion that most other women would have resisted this suffering, but here was this young lady pushing through her dismay and innate self-preservation to get him off in the most devious fashion.

CHAPTER 18

She could only strive to ignore her anguish, striving to maximise his pleasure. Even going so far as to improvise by extending out her tongue as far as she could, chin pushed to her chest, trying to lick the head as it came out of the valley produced by her tied breasts. Something she had seen in those porn flicks.

"You'd best spit on it."

His command a response to the lotion wearing off, forcing his shaft to chafe her flesh. She didn't even ponder now, why she couldn't use more cream. She merely attempted to locate saliva in her dry mouth to embarrassingly trickle across her chest to combine with her tears and perspiration, to aid the glide and spare her some degree of discomfort. Yet still it ached and was aching more and more as she continued on, the longer it took. Her silent tears flowing down her cheeks and over her breasts, the misery she was feeling appearing to crush her own soul, somewhere deep inside.

She was repeating a chant in her thoughts 'Please cum. . . Please cum." Again and over, willing his climax and her rest. Pressing her plump mounds together more firmly and speeding up, she licked desperately at the pistoning tip. She began sobbing and sweating more with her agonising effort, helping provide the lubrication she needed to slide more and more quickly.

Eventually she felt him tense up, the shaft pulse and then shots of his jism flew out onto her chin and neck, hanging for a moment before it dripped back down onto her inflamed breasts. She had to lift her bound breasts off his still firm erection and knowing what he anticipated, she painstakingly licked the combination of come, perspiration, saliva and cream from his cock.

"Please can you take this off? I did what you wanted." She begged anxiously, touching her breasts softly, showing the necklace clasped between them. The sight of her in that position, with her pearl necklace entwined with the gold chain, peering up at him apprehensively from between his thighs, poked at his heart in the afterglow of his huge orgasm.

"You did very well, my little dove" Reaching down, unclipping her rings and letting the pendant dangle between them as a constant reminder of her experience and probable future recurrence.

"Rub my come into your tits."

She obeyed promptly, disregarding the grossness of the act, just grateful her suffering was ended. Without thinking about desire or agony, simply appreciating the comfortable feeling of massaging her painful breasts and firm nips.

After seeing her debase herself, he leant forwards, hands cupping her chin and kissed her lovingly on the lips, merely softly using his lips to rub hers, a stark contrast from the roughness and callousness of the preceding hour.

"You've been a nice girl for me. Thank you" He muttered, his gaze only inches from hers, searching her innermost soul. "Let me run you a refreshing bath and then I'll spread some relaxing after-sun lotion all over your body."

And with that, she sank forwards onto his knees, weeping hysterically, all the emotional intensity of the day pouring through her youthful inexperienced body and overpowering her naïve susceptible mind.

A crippled bird who had survived another storm. In need of leisure and healing, before the next.

He took her to her chamber, small delicate body dangling, wrapped in his muscular arms like a shattered doll, sporadic sobs wrenching her waiflike form. He put her lovingly on the bed and made a bath with calming salts.

Submerging her into the comforting water, he cleaned her hurting body and calmed her receding cries, all the time expressing how proud he was, how unique she was, how much she'd delighted him.

She felt confused, wanting his praise, but hating that he had harmed her so severely for his pleasure, yearning to just be alone to collect her thoughts and the shattered parts of her soul. But she said nothing, just letting him run his hands lightly over her. Incredibly calming for such powerful calloused fingers, the same hands and fingers that had inflicted so much anguish just minutes before.

Outside rain was pouring down, the howling wind of a tropical storm carrying water off the coast. It had started quickly as he put her in the water, echoing the turbulence in her mind. She leapt at the first clap of thunder; her exquisite face highlighted by the flash of lightning.

He pulled her up out of the bath, effortlessly, her small weight no difficulty. Getting her out of danger way, or at least the chance of shock from lightening in the bath. She shuddered, not from cold or dread of the storm outside, but from him and what he had inflicted on her inside.

Drying her in a giant soft cuddly white bath sheet, he wrapped her petite skinny figure with its outsized dimensions and pulled her close and tight in his massive arms, as if shielding her from the storm.

He placed her down on top of the sheets, tenderly massaging after-sun lotion onto her fragile skin. Beginning with her breasts, he delicately calmed the heated skin, stroking the flesh in tiny circles, palming the mound and kneading the cream in between his thumb and fingers in a mild grope, each firm globe a perfect handful.

His massage sent pleasantly lovely feelings through her, washing away the terrible jabs she felt when he touched the bruises and inflammation he had created. Making her angry with her body for responding physiologically to his touch, to the same hands that had injured her so much.

Then caressing her tummy in ever larger circles, sliding softly across her nipples down to her thighs and up her flanks to her neck and then round again. He noticed the goose bumps grow on her sun-reddened skin, as she reacted sensually to his ministrations and the coolness of the cream.

As the cream was absorbed, he seized her hands and lifted them up above her head to overcome the reluctance he sensed in her attentive eyes. Grabbing both her little wrists in one encircling palm, he kissed her, rushing into her mouth, tongue first, smothering any resistance. His insistent tongue spinning around hers, lethargic and non-responsive, imprisoned motionless against her lower jaw in her own mouth. A stubborn sigh was all she could muster.

The fingers of his other hand slipped up to stroke the pale underside of her breasts, then dragging his thumb nail up to her sensitive nips, tugging sensually on the rings. Shocks of fresh pain slicing through her already painful skin and nipples.

He felt the crinkling of the thick skin of her areolae as blood poured into her nub, elongating it and sensitising it even more. Touching every centimetre of the surrounding areola, using his nail to nick every swelling lump. Sending confused signals, unpleasant twinges and pleasurable chills, up her chest, up to her neck, down down her stomach and into her loins.

She grew angry with him, manipulating her, leading her to feel wonderful like this when she simply wanted to despise him. But madder with herself and her body, betraying her with its passionate reaction to his physical manipulation, no matter how hard she attempted to resist. Yet she could not verbalise her fury at him or herself, since she was also terrified. Scared that he would grow even more upset and that he would halt the magnificent feelings racing through her body.

Silently, he slid his mouth down to the lovely puffy nipples and strummed lightly with his tongue.

CHAPTER 19

Circling them with his tongue as he sucked half the solid ball into his mouth, biting softly on the thick skin.

Fireworks exploded in her befuddled thoughts as a burst of light and thunder resonated through the room. That was beautiful and she wanted more. A deepfelt moan vibrating from her throat, her lips locked to prevent its escape.

She couldn't reconcile this delicate sensuous side with the harsh merciless beast that had tormented body and breasts just minutes ago. Seething about the way he drew physical pleasure unwillingly from her breasts with every flick of his tongue and every kiss of his lips. Frustration morphing with arousal in her inexperienced body. Hating him but loathing herself even more for her weakness.

Like the storm outside, the emotional turmoil of her aroused hormones raged against her need to resist him, not to respond to him, to be angry with him, to be alone. He was clutching her hands so tightly that she couldn't move. Couldn't resist. But it felt so amazing. And he had warned her previously that she shouldn't say no, couldn't say no. So, she laid there dumb and let him have his way, again. Using her body like an instrument, with him the consummate musician.

He eased his free hand down to rub her hairless mound in little circles, his fingertips tracing over her skin, but not reaching her genitalia. She had waxed for him before she left for the vacation, like he had ordered her to. Embracing the agony, since he stated it was lovely, it was what he enjoyed. That she had absorbed the ache in her breasts for him. The only difference was the intensity. Waxing was unpleasant, but her breast agony had been awful.

Now he was nibbling on the razor-sharp nipples and sucking the rings onto his tongue, sending off additional explosions. Running his fingernails up and down her inner thighs, to glide over the flesh of her crotch, just besides her vulva, but without touching, just teasing, tickling, scratching. Flashes of anguish and ecstasy, feeling wetness seeping from inside her.

She automatically sought to thrust towards those wonderful fingers, wanting them to touch her core, but he wouldn't allow her and continued to torment the flesh of her inner thighs. Knowing what she had done made her blush in embarrassment and fury, a wanton slut behaving for this manipulative guy, even when he made her feel so uncomfortable.

"Please. . ." She whimpered, passionate, but not really knowing what she was begging for. Whether she wanted him to stop, or whether to satisfy her increasing need.

This was not the clumsy experimentation of the few schoolboys that had felt her up before he had started grooming her. He understood what he was doing and timed every motion to perfection, boosting the surging hormones of this bewildered young girl. Skilled in the sexual domination of countless women, he predicted her response even before she felt it and utilised that to unique advantage.

Gradually, he ran his thumb nail up across her puckered labia towards the protruding clit, sending shockwaves up through her abdomen and into her neck, so strong that she could not breath.

Her eagerness rose as he moved closer, but so did her fury at herself and him, because she didn't want him to touch her there, let alone feel good about it. Yet what her head and heart didn't desire, her sex demanded.

And then his thumb made its initial touch with her clit. Every muscle in her body clenched, back arching, toes curling, fists fisting, neck spasming. Tears of various emotions flowed down her face, wanting to despise the feeling so deeply, yet her body reacting so intensely. Her knees pushed up, broadening to force her pelvis up into his brutal hand. Observing her response, he pulled her knees wider apart with his elbow, massaging her clit aggressively to make her back arch even more.

He stroked his thumb down between her splitting labia finding her rubbery slickness, sending more shockwaves and pyrotechnics through her sensitised body and a frantic mewling from her mouth. Thinking the timing was right, he pushed his thumb inside her sopping quim as another crack of thunder shook the bed. She bucked her hips to meet it, pressing it further, all thoughts of being alone stolen from her with the penetration. His tongue was still circling alternate nipples, licking between them and then biting just hard enough to unleash the endorphins that would enhance her response.

CHAPTER 20

Knowing she was putty in his hands, he no longer had to hold her to have his way. Eager to taste the sweet honey between her legs, he kissed down her slim belly to her pussy. Kissing and probing her glistening vulva, he sent more thrills up her spine, while carefully sliding his thumb in and out of her expanding entrance. She stared down terrified at him sucking her sex, upset at the sensation of embarrassment, thoughts of how unclean, filthy, nasty it was for him to be licking down there. Yet overcome by the wonderful emotions flowing from her loins, sending chills all over her body and lightning through her spirit combining with the storm outside.

Timing it just perfectly he flicked his tongue and nibbled on the small pleasure nub jutting proudly at the top of her slit. He then swallowed the entire mound into his mouth, generating a storm of pleasure in her loins, seeing her face twist in ecstasy, eyes closed as she shook her head from side to side.

"Oooooh myyyyy god!" She had never encountered anything like that in her life. It was not like this when she touched herself, when the schoolboys touched her, even with the vibrator he'd forced her use. The mix of knowledge, power and passion overwhelmed her senses. Gone was any idea of resisting or being by herself. She abandoned herself to the moment and the moment took her. Even when he bit her clit, the flash of pain mixing with her ardour to make the sensations more severe, her feel more alive.

Up and up to a plateau near the gods, where her existence erupted into a thousand shards of light with the lightening outside. He utilised that time to plunge his juice slicked index finger into her anus while continuing to batter her vaginal channel with his thumb, taking even more pleasure from her writhing body. She again was appalled by how unnatural, how disgusting, how repugnant it was to have his finger up her bottom, but yet how nice the sense of fullness felt.

She never envisioned a guy not just placing a finger in her sex but in her ass, so his finger pushed beyond her sphincter before she had a chance to attempt and keep it out. It was instinct that made her clench herself tightly on his finger after it was well inside, cruelly grasping and holding him in, rather than forcing him out. Seeing her fruitless struggle excited him, so he merely kept hard pressure against her holes until she tired of tightening her muscles. When she withdrew, he thrust his finger in even further, assaulting her innocent purity and her self-esteem.

As he rubbed thumb and finger together as he thrust, pressing the tiny membrane together between her two orifices, it seemed like he was touching the depths of her soul. So filthy and repulsive, yet a physical pleasure she didn't know that she could ever experience, nor that another person could offer her.

He'd knelt back up to watch her eyes roll and her body lose control, stroking her sensitive clit with the other hand, her muscles automatically pulsating, twitching and clenching on his entering digits. Her body lost all control to his ministration, becoming multi-orgasmic for the first time in her life in the hands of the experienced older guy.

Her head melted and all she experienced was glorious light and ecstasy, floating on a cloud in heaven. All memories of the torture and pain that he had inflicted, were swept from her mind, as she drifted in the wave of pleasure that he had created.

Still saying nothing, he covered her with a thin blanket, letting her sink into sleep, the sensations and emotions of the day overpowering her fatigued body. Stroking her hair, he stayed with her, holding her, secure against the storm outside and the wrath within, at least for the time.

Afterwards he sat in an armchair, watching and waiting. Considering and pondering his next step. She had shown to be tenacious beyond her years, possibly due to the challenges she had suffered with a distant mother and a missing father. She looked to be so needy and dependent, eager to bear so much in the hope of winning his admiration and attention.

He personally knew the psychology of reliance and desertion, having spent many hours in treatment. Yet that did not offer him empathy for his nude charge, but rather a predatory drive to prey on her weakness, in order to satisfy his own demands.

He rationalised to himself that he was not evil, because he also wanted to protect and nurture. It was only when 'the yearning' emerged, overloading his senses, that he craved more. He had learned to conceive of it as 'the urge', in order to compartmentalise his acts and disconnect from the agony he inflicted. Simply wanting her to surrender and prove her loyalty, her love. Show herself worthy. Accepting whatever he demanded, without question. Seeing how far he could push, before she broke.

And in exchange, he would care for her, protect her, look after her, unconditionally. All while transforming her into the elegant beauty she was destined to be; the hair, the makeup and the wardrobe of a sophisticated young woman. Giving her pleasure in exchange for her suffering, like with this last orgasm, to ensure that the bonds were that much stronger, her need to bring out the caring side forcing her to suffer the cruelty for him.

All while knowing that she had the baby face, dreams and immaturity of a teenage girl, that he could manipulate and control for his own nefarious intent. Other men might be bored with such immaturity and inexperience, but instead he delighted in his complete dominance, made easier by her lack of the knowledge about how to possibly resist.

The next time and every time thereafter, she would have to demonstrate her subjugation to his will. A broken bird that he would strengthen and heal, just to break another wing so she could not fly alone, without him. The sense of power, the affirmation he obtained from her submission, was greater and more satisfying than from any other woman he'd known before.

And now here she was, an innocent canvass in the rough, unadulterated, unopinionated, and unaffected by all the experiences and attitude of older women. They'd been more difficult to mould, to control. Unwilling to suffer as much for him, for his pleasure. Hurting, not because it meant anything, but because he wanted it. As she had surrendered her breasts to him, to use and abuse how he saw fit, regardless of her immediate pain or desires.

He smiled in satisfaction as he watched her sleep, knowing that this was going just the way he'd intended. She had no idea what the next few days would bring, nor that they were going to be earthshattering in terms of the impact they would have on the rest of her life.

She'd shivered and shaken to troublesome dreams in the hour that he watched her, wondering if they had been caused by him or other challenges of her life. Night had fallen and the storm had subsided by the time he quietly left the room, letting her continue sleeping peacefully and rejuvenate so she could be ready for the adventures of the following day.

The sun was already up when she slowly surfaced the next morning, eyes blinking open and darting uncertainly around the room. It had pretty décor, beach cottage chic with white-washed cupboards, a white dressing table, blue stripped curtains, light ash wooden floors and a king size bed with soft pale blue bed linen. All the fittings looked like they were expensive to her inexperienced eye, but it all felt comforting and relaxing.

She had woken briefly during the night and seen that she was alone, but the fatigue and trauma of the day had caused her to drift back into a deep slumber without moving.

CHAPTER 21

He on the other hand, had slept peacefully, risen early, made coffee and gone back into her room to watch her awake.

Her gaze finally came to rest on him, sitting in the light blue upholstered armchair in the corner. A timid smile spread across her face as she focused on him, not saying a word. Her subconscious mind had spent the night processing her experiences of the day and she woke with the self-defensive rationalisation that he did care for her. The rollercoaster of pain, pleasure and emotion was just his way of making her feel intensely alive and desired, and her mood matched the sunshine of the day.

"Hello sleepyhead." His voice gentle and caring as he arose from the chair, moving towards her.

"Morning. . . Ouch, I'm sore all over." The sunburn had gone, but she could feel the aches from her piercings and beating, to the stiffness and strains from her surfing adventure.

"You'll feel better as soon as you start moving." Ignoring her complaints. "I need to treat your piercings, to prevent them from getting infected." Megan the piercer, had been adamant about this the day before and he relished the opportunity to swab and play with her rings.

Pulling the duvet aside he revealed her nakedness. She blushed at his smiling gaze wandering down to her chest and crotch, even though he had seen her naked a thousand times before. Being in the room with him scrutinising her so closely felt way more embarrassing that being on video chat.

He poured alcohol from a small bottle onto a cotton ball, pushed her head unceremoniously to the right and swabbed the three ear studs front and back. It stung but was tolerable and she lay there quietly accepting his right to her body.

Her nipples were a different proposition, the sensitive nubs were throbbing and sensitive from the treatment the day before and twinged painfully when he pulled and twisted on the rings.

"Ouch, they're sore. Please be careful." She pleaded looking at him anxiously. She wasn't certain whether he was doing this out of necessity or just to hurt her. Disinfecting was one thing but twisting and tugging was another. "Do you have to pull so hard?"

"We need to make sure the holes stay clean and open. It's for your own good." Said in an uncompromising tone, without stopping his treatment or looking up from her breast.

He swabbed firmly, while moving the ring around in her sensitive nub, enjoying watching the nipple and surrounding skin pucker from the cold and pain. She just gritted her teeth, surviving this ordeal with a newfound fortitude.

It was just as painful when he doused her belly button with alcohol around the thick gauge post, wriggling it back and forwards as he did so. She scrunched her eyes shut against the sting, a single tear squeezing out of the corner to run slowly across her temple towards her ear, where it disappeared with her resolve.

"It hurts. Please don't be so rough."

"All done." He said cheerfully, before continuing with a hint of enthusiasm. "This morning, we're going for a walk to see the waterfalls and the forest. It's gorgeous and we can swim there. I want to show you the forest and we may see some endangered birds."

"That sounds nice." Unsettled. Eager to try, but. . . "Is it a long way? I'm tired and sore. I don't think I can walk very far."

"You'll be fine. Get up and get dressed. Put these on." He gave her a metallic blue bikini, and dropped a pastel pink cropped shirt with white lace trim, cut-off jeans and leather sandals on the bed. He leant against the chair, waiting and watching her inspect the clothes before pulling the bikini top over her head and sliding the bottom up her legs. She had to wriggle them on, because they were really tight and form fitting, the bottom being a thong and the top more of a low-cut sports bra.

"Hold on. Just one addition before you finish dressing." He strode over to her, pulling something round and silver out of his pocket and holding it up. With a shock, she realised it was a princess butt-plug, like the one he had made her buy, but slightly larger and with a bright blue gem glinting on the base.

"What? Why'd you have that?" Not willing to believe that he wanted her to put that thing inside herself. When they were going for a walk?

"Because I want you to wear it. And you're my girl." His tone definite. "Anyway, it's no different to what you've become used to."

"But I don't want to. Please?" Her voicing taking on a whining edge.

She hated the plug, ever since he had made her shove it in her bottom the first time. Oiling it up and pressing as hard as she could, while he was watching and encouraging her through the video feed. She recalled the pain and the pressure, not getting her sphincter to accommodate its inch diameter and not comprehending why he would want her to put something up there in the first place.

Later making her stick an oiled finger in, then two, feeling so embarrassed and dirty. But his persistent encouragement ensuring that she obeyed his demands.

Then the vibrator to 'loosen her up." Making her turn it on so that a weird humming sensation spread through her crotch, making her feel good down there but in an odd full sort of a way. The pleasure conflicting with her sense that nothing should go up in there.

Yet with his tuition, she had learned to push out when shoving things in, to assist them overcome the tight ring that naturally blocked her most secret place from invasion.

But he didn't let her keep it private, pushing her to spread herself wide, legs held up in a V so that he could see what she was doing and give her directions. Or on her broad knees, back arched and chest down, forcing things into herself for his enjoyment, flushing scarlet into the pillow, horrified at how she must seem. Furious with herself for craving his attention so much that she debased herself for him. But not doing anything with that emotion, except supressing it in frustration while she performed his bidding.

CHAPTER 22

After a few days of 'practise' as he termed it, he made her try the plug again. This time the practise paid off as she understood to push out as it gently slid in, expanding her tight hole her wider and wider. It was uncomfortable and demeaning to have to do that to herself with him looking, so she couldn't gaze at the screen as he wanted.

But suddenly it was in and her asshole constricted to clutch the slender shaft. The anguish switched to a fullness she had not expected and there was her behind ornamented with a pink glass bead, rather than the tight tiny anal star that she was used to seeing. He forced her hold it in for an hour that first time, before he commanded her to draw it back out, gently stretching her rectum outwards as her skin stretched the opposite way, hurting just as much as on the way in.

When she grew used to it, she would have to keep it in for much longer and even go out with it under her clothing. Reporting back to him how she felt about it. She would tell him how uncomfortable it was, how full it made her feel and how embarrassing to have to wear it, never getting used to the feeling, even when it ceased being painful.

But not getting used to the guilt of having to lick it for lubrication, attempting to slaver saliva on the bulb to ease it into her dry hole and prevent too much discomfort. It is always stretched a bit going in and out, regardless of how much she had to use it.

She mistakenly assumed he wanted her to keep it as a display of his power, which she had entirely handed over to him by then. Little did she know his genuine motive, but she was going to find out that day.

"Stop being foolish and lube it up." Placing it in front of her lips, expecting her to take it in, his other hand enveloping the back of her swanlike thin neck. She did as he requested, gazing at him with a mixture of wrath and misery, sucking it and creating as much spit as she could, from experience understanding how it would aid her.

"Okay. That's enough." Rotating her and pulling down on her neck. "Bend over. Back arched. Legs straight. . ." All business now, he hooked a finger into the top of her bottoms above her crack and tugged them down to just below her cheeks, revealing the spot he desired. Without hesitating, he placed the tip of the silver bulb against her tight anal ring. She instantly clinched hard, fighting the entrance.

"Relax. . . You know how." And with that command the plug made steady progress against the tight hole, stretching it wider and wider, the burning sensation intensifying, even as she battled the desire to squeeze it out. She wriggled her bottom from side to side to try and make the agony go away or the plug to slip out, but all that she managed to do was to work it farther in

Once it reached to the widest area, it was almost as if her sphincter couldn't expand any farther and she clamped down, trying to reject the intruder. But he was not going to be stopped and sustained the pressure such that her anal muscles only succeeded in drawing it into her ass, the skin stretched pallid before recovering its colour as it compressed back around the shaft. Out of the corner of his vision he caught the surprised expression on her face peering at him over her shoulder, as she felt the big size penetrate her narrowest hole.

"Oooooooh. It's so enormous. I can't walk with this in. Please take it out." Dismay flooding her as he tugged the thong back up to draw taught over the plug, displaying glimpses of the blue jewel around the edges of the thin matching blue strap of material.

"That looks sexy. Get ready and then we need to get a bite to eat before we depart. You need to maintain your strength up." He smirked smugly and slapped her rear, before storming out of the room without a second glance.

She took a long breath, pondering whether to defy him. She simply wanted the fullness in her intestines to be gone but didn't want to upset him, having experienced what he was capable of. Her trip home was the next day. She decided she could manage this for today.

Sighing deeply, she took up the shorts and slid them up her legs. They were so short and tight that the crotch was simply a small strip of tattered material that slipped up into her crack, allowing her buttocks to protrude out cheekily, even while she was standing. She didn't want to think about what it would look like if she leant over, because they pressed snuggly against her pussy and pushed against up the plug in her ass.

The crop top was similarly a snug fit, supporting her breasts firmly while displaying a faint raised outline of her nips and rings. Her bare stomach showcased her shiny new navel ring.

She glanced at herself in the bedroom mirror, little ashamed by the exposed nature of the garments, but also conflicted by being delighted at how grown up and seductive she appeared. And how much he'd appreciate it, particularly with the thrust of her arse and arch of her back to fit the bulb filling her bottom.

She moved gingerly to the kitchen, attempting to reduce the suffering. He had offered her drinks and breakfast again and she ate standing up, not wanting to sit on the plug if she didn't have to.

"Is my flight planned for tomorrow?" She questioned, that being top of mind and having counted on him to organise all the specifics for the trip. On the way there, he had just emailed her boarding permit and she arrived at the check-in with her bogus ID with everything ready.

"I looked earlier and there seems to be a problem with the web site" He told the falsehood without hesitation. "Don't worry, we'll straighten things up when we come back later."

"Okay. I hope it's alright." Hesitantly, wondering what may be wrong. "Maybe I should call my mum. To let her know I'm okay."

"It wouldn't be a good idea." He responded. "You told her you were going on to visit a buddy. She's not expecting you to call. Nevertheless, your former phone carrier doesn't have service here and we can't risk you utilising the smartphone."

CHAPTER 23

"I think you're correct." Taking it everything at face value. Then looked around the home. "Whose house is this? Is it yours? It's absolutely wonderful."

"No. It's a friend's." Smiling reassuringly. "He lets me use it when I'm here. Come on. Eat up and let's get moving. The hike is very wonderful. Exactly like you. You'll light up the surroundings looking like that."

"Please can I take it out. It's really unpleasant." Looking at him uncomfortably. Then hope to negotiate a bargain. "I'll put it in when we get back, if you want. Please."

His hand flew out, swift as a rattlesnake, grasping her throat in a pincer-like hold. Squeezing and pushing her up and towards him so that just her toes were touching the ground. Most of her weight held up by his firm hold surrounding her weak neck, adding the pressure to her throat, making breathing difficult.

"Haven't I instructed you to do what I say?" He hissed looking daggers into her eyes, scaring the little fragile girl. She couldn't react verbally with pressure on her throat, but mouthed 'yes' with a timid nod.

"Then stop whining, else I may be compelled to reprimand you. . . You don't want that. Do you?" His statements earning a small shake of her head and a 'no'. Eyes large in her little face, as she tried to get oxygen into her lungs.

"Good. Then let's go." His voice returning to normal, as he shut off a light. He let her down and eased his grasp but stayed holding her to keep her from falling. Wrapping his hand around behind her neck, he marched her determinedly to the car and forced her into the passenger seat.

As she sat, the plug burrowed deeper into her intestines, reminding her exactly how huge it was and how full she felt. But she was not going to make another statement about it and sat there demurely chewing her bottom lip as it shifted painfully with every bump in the road.

This time she remained silent while he drove, listening to him lecture her about the historical and spiritual value of the location. Being interested by history, she absorbed what he was saying and nearly forgot about the object inside her.

He paid the admission fee and they started the three-quarter mile trek up to the falls and the pool where they could swim. The forest and palm trees where gorgeous and he told her all about the ancient structures and plants, as he dragged her along, securely clutching her hand, fingers linked like lovers.

As they strolled by other people on the route, she observed the lusty and envious expressions of the older guys, identical to those she got at home when he made her dress sexy. It made her ashamed that people assumed that he was not her father, but rather her boyfriend. Watching them ogling her also sent thrills up her spine and a tingle between her legs. The bulb in her accommodating rear made her feel so full while rubbing beautifully into her crotch to add to those sensual feelings.

But it was the older women's critical glares that she felt the most, shaking their heads and even mumbling under their breath, targeted largely at him, for they merely looked at her with pity. She wondered if they could tell that she had a butt-plug, based on the way she was walking, bottom out and toes pointed slightly in to avoid the worst discomfort and minimise the rubbing of the base and shaft on her flesh. That notion made her blush with humiliation as they strolled along.

The young folks didn't appear to care, being wrapped up in their own business. She regarded them with a degree of jealousy, wondering what it would be like to be normal. Whatever normal was. And it made her question whether she would truly like it, because as he had said 'normal was dull' and she always felt so tremendously thrilled and alive with him, even if it was awful and painful occasionally.

As they went, he pointed out different trees and the old structures, explaining their value and diverting her from the lecherous and judging stares. The birds produced a magnificent symphony of chirping as soundtrack to the walk. He joyfully showed her a rare night heron, sitting on a tree overhead, which warmed her to this mysterious man who could be so nasty and yet care so much.

"Strip off. We're going to jump in and have a swim." He told her after they reached the pool, underneath the gorgeous waterfall.

There were many people surrounding the pool, making her feel exceedingly self-conscious about the swimmers and the item inside her that it scarcely covered. She loved the metallic blue colouring, however it was just to little and tight.

"Get on with it." He remarked severely, pulling off his own shirt down to his board shorts.

She said nothing as she removed her shoes and blouse, before gently pulling down her shorts, making sure to facing way from the other people, so as not to not bend over and expose anybody her humiliating secret. She had to stand up straight and tighten her buttocks as she rapidly stepped onto the water, ensuring that the glinting stone would not peep out, but at the same time forcing it to be dragged farther into her belly.

He embraced her in a strong hug once she was up to her neck in the water and carried her over to the far side of the pond, too deep for her to stand. She had never felt comfortable in water where she couldn't stand, and this was no exception. She felt both scared floating in the water and safe in his arms, the contradicting sensations causing butterflies to flutter in her belly.

His hands wandered into her top, exposing one of her breasts beneath the water and fondling it possessively, reminding her of how badly he had damaged it the day before. These were not the hands of a fumbling eager youngster, but rather the calm mature hands of an experienced man who pressed them to the point of agony, sending confused messages through her body, owning and directing her response. Understanding how to touch her nipples and twist her rings just right to make them quickly firm, like stones in the chilly ocean. Sending tingling feelings across her body, sensually blending with the smooth swirling and lapping of the water against her flesh.

His second hand crept inside the front of her thong, casually fingering her slit and teasing her clit. She looked around nervously to check if anybody was watching. Thankfully, the family on the opposite side of the pond were self-absorbed, with the parents grilling and the little son and daughter playing in the shallows. The lone man sitting on a bench was hunting for birds in the woods, binoculars diverting his attention elsewhere.

There were a few other couples also floating in the water, one kissing and the other laughing at a private joke. None of these kept her from feeling ashamed as he had his way with her in public, without considering her wishes, needs, views or sensibilities. Nor did it stop her deceitful pussy from warming and juicing up for him, despite her best attempts to resist. His chilly fingers opened her heated folds, allowing the cold water into her sex, eddying over her sensitive lips and across her engorged clit, washing away her wetness, leaving her damp. Hot and cold at the same moment, reflecting her conflicted feelings, internal desire tinged with public shame.

They reached a big boulder that barely pierced the surface of the water. It was partly coated in slimy moss, while the other areas were harsh to the touch. He pulled her forwards till she was wedged against the rock, feet not touching the bottom of the water. Her anxiety at floating freely in the water, slightly assuaged by clinging onto the rock, but not enough to feel safe.

CHAPTER 24

He had yanked her top up so now both breasts were hanging out below the water, smashed up with her stomach on the abrasive rock, her delicate pierced nipples viciously scraped. Her legs had no grip on the slick moss and her feet flailed seeking to gain hold on the bottom that was only inches out of reach. She felt like a rag doll bouncing about fully at his mercy.

She tried to hold herself stable by grabbing the flat surface above the water, but there were no handholds and her forearms and fingers hung on by friction alone, creating microscopic grazes on her fragile skin. Her wet hands merely made the rock even more slippery, so they slid about ineffectively, not helping her state of mind nor her concealed unease.

His forearm was firmly forced into her back, palm around her petite neck, trapping her like an insect on a display. Suddenly she felt him tug the strap of her swimming suit to the side, exposing her ass crack and the butt plug to a swirl of chilly water.

"What are you doing?" She muttered in amazement and a touch of terror.

"I'm going to fuck you up the ass." He snarled; the passion apparent in his harsh tone as the monster she had come to know was released. He had tugged his shorts down so now she could feel his erection lined up in the crevice of her butt

"Please, you can't. Not here. Not like this. Please take me home. I'll let you do it there. Please." She couldn't comprehend how he could expect her to lose her anal virginity in public, up against a rock. She started trying, but he was too powerful, and she couldn't get any traction to push against him, with him standing solid on the sandy bottom. Her legs and arms merely flailing ineffectually, trying not to move too furiously and draw any notice from the other individuals spread about the pond.

"Shut the fuck up and get ready. It's not what you'll let me do. It's what I want to do. Remember?" As he talked, he drew the plug out of her asshole, the stretching making it hurt and letting a stunning stream of cold water into her intestines. "You've been practising with the dildo, so it should be simple."

She froze in dread, thinking there was nothing she could do to stop him. Wondering why he wanted to demean her and humiliate her all the time. Particularly after he had been so thoughtful and considerate. Her naïve, inexperienced intellect not being able to reconcile the paradox.

"Open your mouth." He hissed as he placed the plug at her lips.

"Mmmmh mmmh." She didn't want it in there. Even though it was soaking with water the notion of where it had been disgusted her. He had forced her suck her butt-plug off once on tape, but it disgusted her, and she had refused subsequently.

He wasn't interested in her fruitless struggle, wasn't going to debate the subject and had no desire to postpone his passion any longer, so instead he inserted his hard cock at her tight puckered entrance and pushed firmly.

"Aaaaaahhhgggg..." Her groan was suppressed as he closed her lips with the horrible silver bulb, while the bulb of his glans pierced her tight hole. The fury at being simultaneously entered from both ends, in such as filthy repulsive fashion, yet with no method of avoiding it destroyed the young woman. She fell, pressed against the rock, little tears pouring down her cheeks as he drove more into her and held the plug firmly in her mouth.

She was convinced she could taste the harsh tanginess of her ass as the plug forced her tongue down and strained against her palate, pushing towards her neck, painfully filling her oral cavity like it had filled her rectal canal only seconds before. It blended with the dank earthy organic fragrance of the pondwater, penetrating her nostrils, particularly when a splash of water from his push splashed her face and went up her nose, forcing her to choke and sputter around the thing in her mouth.

"It'll help you remain quiet when I screw you." He spoke with no remorse. "You should hold it in and remain quiet, because I'm sure you don't want those folks to know what you're doing." He chuckled at the final comment, but obviously without amusement as he proceeded to shove up into her intestines.

His turgid rock-hard member strained her anal ring, so she imagined that she could feel every vein and bump on his organ, even though the taught skin burned with anguish. She relaxed in self-defence, attempting to decrease the dreadful agony and stuffed sensation, but all that permitted was for him to breach the opening until he was balls-deep in her rectum.

She felt every inch of penetration as his cock scratched the fragile walls of her intestines, where nothing like this was designed to go or had gone before. Tears of fury were running down her cheeks, quietly crying but no less devastating that if she was screaming her heart out. Even her cries meant nothing to him nor the pond, as they were rinsed away by the sprays of water on her face when he positioned her for his use. Utilizing her buoyancy in the water, her incapacity to grip anything and not stand on the bottom, to his advantage.

Repulsed by the horror of her situation, held against the boulder, tart smelling plug in her mouth, queasy bile in her throat, filthy pondwater in her nostrils, rough cock up her bottom, she couldn't do anything to stop him. He continued beating away at her, her stomach, breasts and arms being scraped against the hard rock, without achieving much constructive in her defence.

At first it was merely painful, but as he persisted, the various minor abrasions started burning and aching more and more. Her nipple and naval rings snagged on the rock, feeling like they were being purposely yanked, sending sharp needles of pain to add to her general anguish.

She saw that her fingernails were holding the rock like a climber trying to summit El Capitain, seeking for any foothold on the granite face, almost as in slow motion. Everything had gone silent, her entire consciousness reduced to the anguish of a pole in her ass and the scrape of her flesh. Suffering the firm man flesh plunging into her depths, moistened by the surrounding water and feeling every vein and bump sliding against her stretched anal ring and walls.

CHAPTER 25

Then abruptly gazing up, with the noises and scents of the world slamming back into her senses: birds tweeting, children laughing, leaves rustling, the damp stink of the pond and the fragrance of the flowers. Letting her believe that she was small in the bigger cosmic order and her experience was irrelevant in the greater scheme of things.

As though even objects as inert as the rock and the water, colluded against her, enabling his abuse of her, his exploitation of her. Letting him to drive into her private location a thousand times over, with her not having any say, nor control. In reality, removing whatever control she may have had on dry land, so that she was a helpless puppet swinging on a thread, or more appropriately dancing on a pole.

All she could do was accept what he provided, hoping that he would finish fast and let it be done. She started tightening her bottom on his cock on the out stroke, thinking it would stimulate him and make him cum. And while she growled with every stroke, she managed to keep her pained moans low enough that no one else could hear.

Cold water trickled into her rear with every thrust, her dilating sphincter not insuring a tight enough fit with his violent fucking. It felt bizarre and terrible, contrasting to the heat of his prick, blending with the bodily and mental suffering from his thoughtless abuse of her limited power and lack of desire to resist.

She sat there loathing him for his harshness and despising herself for her vulnerability, but it made little difference to the end.

The family and lovers continued on blissfully ignorant, caught up in their own delight, as she was assaulted and devastated only yards away. Nevertheless, the man on the bench had spotted them and began to observe them through his binoculars, which simply added to her sadness. The smirk on his face made it evident that he understood precisely what they were doing and definitely approved, particularly when he put his hand into his pocket presumably to rub himself to her ravishment.

The physical pleasure, his sense of dominance over her, and his awareness of the suffering and humiliation she was undergoing for him quickly led to his release, depositing a big load of sperm deep into her intestines.

In contrast to the frigid water that had made its way into her swollen intestines, she felt the warm flood of his sperm permeate her depths. She experienced no sense of relief, excitement, or fulfillment. Nothing except misery, suffering, and despair.

As soon as he had cum, he immediately removed the plug from her lips. He pushed the plug back into her ravished asshole as he made his way out of her asshole.

It was wonderful. He exulted. "Let's return home."

He was thinking about what had happened during the previous few of hours while he was driving. She sat glumly and motionless, lost in her own thoughts, sometimes giving him a scathing stare while gazing out the window of the automobile.

He found it amazing and definitely something to repeat to take her anal virginity in public while she writhed frantically between that rock and his erect cock. Her asshole clenching so desperately for his cum, her pitiful pleading moans muffled by the butt-plug in her mouth, her body trembling from his assault and the abrasion on her breasts, her futile attempts to resist his far superior strength, her innocent wriggling movements to avoid pain that increased his enjoyment, and her obvious humiliation at the public act, with the birdwat, all tickled his sexual desires.

Even though she had fought against his encircling arms on the trip back to the beach, due to his power and her wish to keep their battles private, he had floated her back in a similar fashion to how they had gone to the rock. Under the water, he is still firmly mauling and pinching her nipple with one of his hands.

Before getting dressed, she cleansed her face in an effort to cover her colored crying eyes and heated cheeks. She was cautious not to over-button her shorts or allow the tight top irritate her chaffed chest as she put it over her head.

In a parody of the walk they had taken to the pool, he grasped her hand and held it firmly in the same lover's grasp as when they had arrived, dragging her reticent but yielding body behind him. She was unable to resist him because of her immaturity, which was evident in the maelstrom of intense emotions racing through her small body.

She was obviously disgusted with him, his wants, and her inability to rebuff him. She was also visibly irate, disappointed, saddened, and ashamed. On their rapid walk back to the car, these feelings ran over her face both separately and together. Her small legs had to virtually run to keep up with him.

Although this pouting young girl act was grating on his nerves, he was glad to have the time to reflect since he had some significant decisions to make in the upcoming 24 hours. He had had enough by the time they arrived at the villa.

"Stop acting so young. You are a stunning woman with incredible elegance and sensuality. When they walked inside the front door, he lectured. Guys desire women who they can possess, enjoy, and nurture. I enjoyed giving you the boot. And I really enjoyed doing it in front of all those people. Sharing deep closeness was thrilling, risky, and depraved—all the things that make us feel truly alive. You will eventually come to enjoy it as well. Just quit whining and mature.

"Hmmm!" She muttered, and when he gave her a hopeful look as though expecting a response, she muttered again. "I won't ever like it. It stung.

He gave a patronizing smile. "Just the initial few occasions. Most females learn to like it. Bending the truth while in her innocence being unsure about her thoughts.

CHAPTER 26

"When you act like that, you're an animal. Why did you need to be so vicious? I believed you to like me. She complained, but with a stern expression on her face.

Ah, little tiny dove. I really enjoy you. You are the ideal woman for me. She was taken aback by his sudden candor and sympathetic tone, but he interrupted her before she could respond, saying, "I'm going for a brief surf. I anticipate a more positive disposition and less whining when I return. This afternoon, we're going to do something incredibly enjoyable.

For you, I wager. She responded rudely, but she soon proceeded after noticing a moment of rage in his eyes. "Sorry. . ."

He just turned and left. She ascended the veranda after him like a scared puppy dog. He took up his surfboard and she inquired hesitantly. Please double-check my flight for tomorrow.

All she could think about at the time was returning home, to her mother and her dull, routine existence. He believed that in order to "feel truly alive" or "experience profound closeness," one had to go through what she didn't believe she really wanted to.

"I did. Earlier. It appears to have been postponed. Later, we'll give another call. abrupt, final, and careless in his manner. "Oh absolutely. And if you wish, you may remove the plug. Unless you want to wait till tomorrow to let it out. He made the remark while grinning as he proceeded down the trail.

Before gently making her way into the home, she merely stood there and gazed dejectedly as he turned and retreated. She had never been left alone before, and all she wanted to do was return home, so she wasn't sure what to do.

After spending the hour in the waves reflecting and finding his center, he came back feeling renewed, energised, and satisfied with himself. She spent a half hour attempting to remove the sensation of dirt and degradation from her body and her bottom before taking a shower and changing into a comfortable light green dress and white shoes. She was missing a butt plug.

They were in the kitchen together after a brief shower when he pulled out his phone to check for missed calls or texts. A blocked call to her home state reinforced the worried look he had caught out of the corner of her eye from her. Evidently, she tried to make a call before realizing that while she could unlock the phone with his PIN, she was unable to make any calls or wipe any records without his fingerprint.

She wasn't sure whether he knew that she had been outed. She saw him looking at his phone but saying nothing while fear tore at her gut. Perhaps he didn't notice.

He gave the impression that he had not noticed while warmly grinning, looking her in the eye, and speaking. "This afternoon, I'm taking you out on my boat for a sunset cruise because I'm so proud of you and what you've allowed me to accomplish. We'll attempt to spot dolphins or perhaps even a whale.

With those words, I was able to stifle my pent-up anxiety over being discovered, my desperation about not making it home, and the trials of the previous couple of days. She has always been fascinated by dolphins and whales; she watches documentaries about them and prints out images of them for her walls. She imagined seeing them in the wild one day and even swimming with them.

And he was aware of this desire thanks to their numerous conversations. His knowledge and expertise of the water had been such an appeal for the young woman that she had often asked him questions and was a vital source of her adoration for him.

I see, truly. I want to see that. She gushed, almost as if she had forgiven or forgotten everything else.

"We'll make a pit break en route and have lunch at a restaurant I know." He took a pink object from his pocket. She thought it seemed to be two balls joined in the shape of an hourglass with a sting on one side.

While she had never seen anything like that, when she heard what he said, her heart fell. You must first do something for me, though. Come on in. She approached him carefully, her face glowing with worry. Bend over, as in

I beg you not to harm me once more. She bowed over the counter as he ordered, but she was troubledly staring back at him.

"It won't hurt at all," he said. Believe me. She was unsure about her thoughts. He had never really told her lies. He just twisted the truth. And he had given her terrible anguish and shame. Yet for the time being, she could see no other option except to listen and trust that he was being truthful.

She had chosen a gorgeous pair of green pants to go with her outfit, and he was happy with her choice as he flipped up her short skirt to admire her toned thighs and firm buttocks. He put his balls to her mouth but said nothing. She became aware that this object was entering her body and that she should lubricate it.

I really hoped it wouldn't be in her underwear. She was upset that she was scared, annoyed that she was ignorant, expecting the worst, realizing that she had little control over the situation, and choosing not to say anything that might enrage him. attempting to focus just on dolphins and whales.

He pushed her pants apart and placed his finger on her sealed clam as she was sucking on the object that was filling her lips with its rubbery flavor and scent. To feel for any moisture, he softly rubbed inside her labia while he slowly separated her.

He was unaffected by the fact that she was closed off and had not been aroused in the previous few hours. He just kept exploring her hole, almost delicately gliding up and down her delicate lips, till he discovered traces of her undesired response on the tip of his finger.

She hoped that this indicated that the object was entering her vagina. She was annoyed that he had such complete control over her treacherous body that he could cause her to juice up so rapidly, even though she knew it would help.

He positioned it at her entry and pushed the Ben Wa balls into her passageway when they were both covered in her saliva and her essence, gradually filling her and forcing her muscular walls to tighten around the invasion.

He gave her a slap on the back and remarked matter-of-factly as he abruptly slid the panties back in place to confine the intruder within. "Let's leave."

They were seated at a window at a tiny café with a view of the ocean thirty minutes later. She had never experienced anything like it before when she was walking, and the inside sex pleasure had been tremendously distracting. But as usual, he was not interested in taking his time and dragged her along, making sure that the balls did their job and that by the time they sat down, she was dripping dampness into her panties.

He gave them orders once again and started describing the regulations of the yacht to her. He pulled out his phone, grinned enigmatically, and opened an app while speaking.

Her mouth began to form a quiet "Oh" as her eyes enlarged. She hunched over and appeared to be in discomfort. Instead of agony, she felt a pulsating vibration deep inside her instead. That had such an odd, yet wonderful, feeling. She said, "What?" in a voice she didn't trust.

"Yes. Those are Ben Wa balls and will make you very happy. When we eat, I'm going to play with them. You're going to act as if nothing is happening. He stopped before muttering inanely conspiratorially while flashing a sarcastic grin. Unless you want to tell the waiter anything, of course.

CHAPTER 27

He played with her as they waited for the food and while they were eating it, conversing casually the entire while. He would increase the pressure until she was trembling, gasping for air, and feeling as like she was ready to hit a crescendo as all she could think about was the pleasure and the direct stimulation of her g-spot. He would turn it off before she did, allowing her desire to wane as he talked to her about routine maritime safety concerns.

When he noticed that she had calmed, he would start speaking once again, distracting her and slowing down her eating so that she couldn't focus on what he was saying. It repeatedly occurred, leaving her feeling exhausted and horny from not being able to get relief.

She attempted to sneakily place her hands between her legs once, but he shook his head and pretended to summon the waiter over instead. She was more and more irritated with herself and her receptive body, which she didn't seem to be able to control. Why couldn't she fight back when he tried to physically or emotionally harm her?

She became enraged with him for continuing to abuse her in this way, but she was powerless to stop the torrent from oozing from her overstimulated pussy. She was even more embarrassed and enraged when she realized that she was probably soaking the back of her dress.

Ultimately she threatened "Stop it. I'm going to the restroom to get rid of this, so kindly excuse me.

He looked at her with a deadpan expression as he turned the dial to the maximum vibration before answering quietly. So I might not be here when you come back, I said.

Her bluff was called, her shoulders sagged, and she silently endured the subsequent cycle of arousal and repression. He finally let her go over the brink and into a mind-shattering orgasm with her last mouthful of a wonderful crème brulee.

She was speechless other than a small squeak from deep within her throat, her eyes rolling back and her face contorted in ecstasy. It appeared to anybody observing, in a fashion reminiscent of "When Harry met Sally," that the desert was actually unique.

He purposefully followed her as they got up from the table to cover the wet spot on the back of her dress. While the balls themselves were silent and motionless inside of her, their walking-related feelings were not.

They soon climbed aboard his 54-foot ocean-going boat, and he instructed her on how to assist him in casting off. He could sail alone because the boat was fully computerized, but he wanted her to be occupied and preoccupied while they were still in port.

As they sped out of the yacht club marina and into the great blue sea, she couldn't help but comment on everything she was seeing since she was still a little girl inside, full of excitement. She enjoyed standing at the bow and searching for shallow outcrops while assisting with mainsail raising.

As three dolphins joined them in riding the bow wave for a short while, her eyes twinkled and she couldn't contain her childlike joy. She felt as though her heart would burst with joy as the day's events, her disappointments, and her fears were washed away by the moving marine life.

He gave her instructions once they were offshore and under sail. "Go into a bikini down there. They'll be in the cabin up front.

"Really? Are there extra bikinis on board? She was shocked and questioned who they were.

"Go on. You'll notice. Standing up behind the wheel and looking out to sea, he gave a cryptic response.

She reappeared a little while later with a perplexed look on her face, wearing a red bikini and a multicolored sarong knotted around her waist.

"The cabin is packed with all of my clothing. What is happening? The Darkness of Desire, the first epilogue

"The cabin is packed with all of my clothing. What is happening? I'm not required to pretend any more. He barked. You foolish little slut, you attempted to call your mother. That was a careless act.

She was in his hands as he spoke, along with a spare rope that was coiling in the cockpit, ready for him to use. She was on her knees and her hands were bound behind her back within seconds as he fastened her wrists to her ankles. She was paralyzed and chafed by the wires as she peered up at him in awe.

CHAPTER 28

"I didn't.. I didn't. I didn't even attempt to call her. With his sudden shift in attitude, she stumbled in amazement and terror. I made an attempt to contact my pal by phone. To explain to her, to stand in for me, etc. because of the delayed flight.

No matter who you tried to call, I don't care. You never call without my approval. As he was still speaking, he tore the dress in the front, yanked it off her shoulders, and caused it to gather over her tied wrists and around her hips.

"From now, just say what I instruct you to say with your mouth. And I'm going to use it to fuck your throat so you can learn that lesson. long and difficult Without even attempting to unbuckle the belt, he had forced his enraged dick through the fly of his shorts.

You fucking mouth, open. Now." He spoke in a frantic tone. When I whip your tits and your ass, the remainder of your punishment will be 10 times worse, so you'd best attempt to please me.

The worst choking episode she had ever had occurred when he seized her head in two hands and rammed his hard member right down her throat and into her mouth. He continued pounding her throat without taking into account her need for air or her hushed cries. Her little hands writhe in despair, powerless.

He finally felt pleased that the lesson had been understood and that he had merited his prize. He pressed her lips on his crotch while leaving a belt buckle mark on her forehead till he felt his balls contract. He withdrew and sprayed numerous loads all over her face in four quick strokes. She was covered with oozing cum, across her forehead and into her hair, across her lips and face, one going up her nose that set off, her sniffing and sneezing.

She was hunched over, retching, and weeping in sorrow as she knelt there, wondering how things could have gone so wrong. After finishing, he lifted her by her hair and looked at her with icy, ruthless eyes.

Your belongings remain in the cabin since you are staying there rather than returning home, His eyes and speech are both emotionless. You're coming with me to the Pacific Islands, I promise. to act as my slut and do anything I please, whenever I please, and whatever I please. for whatever long I desire. After that, I'll determine how to treat you. She had never heard him speak with such malice in the past.

He paused before ending with a chilly, humorless laugh. "I've merely been playing along to assess your suitability as an obedient little sex slave. Let's now begin with your punishment. Consider it the beginning of your training.

His words tore at her spirit, twisting her heart. The kind lover she had hoped for instead of the beast she dreaded had emerged from this guy she had come here to be with. He had always been Mr. Hyde.

It's over

"The cabin is packed with all of my clothing. What is happening?

"I saw you attempted to call home. Little dove, it was really dumb.

He ignored her query and shifted the conversation's attention with a voice tinted with repressed rage.

"I didn't attempt to call her," the speaker said. She stumbled as she worried about being discovered and his potential wrath. "I attempted to contact my pal by phone. to ask her to stand in for me. because of the delayed flight.

"That isn't the issue. That implies that I can't rely on you. His words pierced her heart like a dagger. That implies that I should move a bit more quickly. I'll take care of your punishment later. In the meanwhile, I'll let you choose between two radically different destinies.

He loomed over her menacingly, making her back away yet keep her gaze fixed on his piercing eyes. Despite their wrathful fire, she believed she saw tenderness in them, but she wasn't certain. She used good judgment by remaining silent and trying to figure out what he was talking about.

"As I've already told you, you're a fantastic girl. You'll develop into a beautiful woman. I would like to participate in, direct, and enjoy that adventure. But in order to achieve it, I need your full obedience. You must comply with my wishes at all times, at any location, and perhaps even with whoever I choose. I'll be your guide while you examine your darkest sexual dreams and concerns. Your surrender to my judgments.

She was horrified as she stared at him and believed that whether she wanted it or not, he was going to kidnap her. Because of this, he had her baggage. How could she have been so foolish to come here alone, to trust him?

He carried on in a serious tone. "In return, I'll make sure you receive the greatest education possible. Via letters throughout the course of the ensuing years as we cruise the Pacific Islands. Afterwards, if you choose, I will cover your tuition at whatever university you are accepted to worldwide. But you have to give me your total, undivided attention. Body, soul, heart, and mind. You can email your mum one time to let her know you've fled and are fine. She can receive one from you every six months to let her know you're okay.

He gave her a moment to process her confusing feelings and ideas before speaking in a little more forceful tone. "If you choose not to accept, then. I'll send you off at the airport tomorrow, and after that, I won't ever get in touch with you again. In any case, a thorough throat fucking will be the punishment for your transgression. After that, you can keep me company in my bed tonight. Within an hour, please respond."

She was unable to comprehend the significance of what he was saying or its effect on her life. She was immediately forced to her knees and had the hard organ she had become accustomed to removed before she had a chance to ponder. He violently thrust it into her mouth and down her throat, beating her till he discharged it directly into her abdomen.

He abandoned her on the ground, hunched over, gasping and crying, reflecting on how he had treated her throat and the ultimatum he had issued. Whether to stay and secure her educational future through perhaps untold torture over the next few years or to return home to relative safety with long-term doubt about her future.

He discreetly steered the boat, establishing a course on a heading that she was not aware of, while she sat on the deck and looked out into the dusk light darkening over the water. Considering significant, life-altering choices that no youngster should be forced to make.

Was it truly plausible that he was mostly Dr. Jekyll with brief periods of Mr. Hyde? Or was she playing Eliza Doolittle and he was really Professor Higgins from Pygmalion?

She turned to her reading for advice on any significant changes in her young life. Nonetheless, there were mostly open-ended questions rather than many conclusive solutions.

Long after that, he asked plainly while seated next to her. What choices have you made?

THE END

CPSIA information can be obtained
at www.ICGtesting.com
Printed in the USA
BVHW040741300323
661444BV00001B/6